UP NEXT...

on **Sports Illustrated KIDS**

:02 SPORTS ZONE SPECIAL REPORT

:04 **FEATURE PRESENTATION:**

END ZONE THUNDER

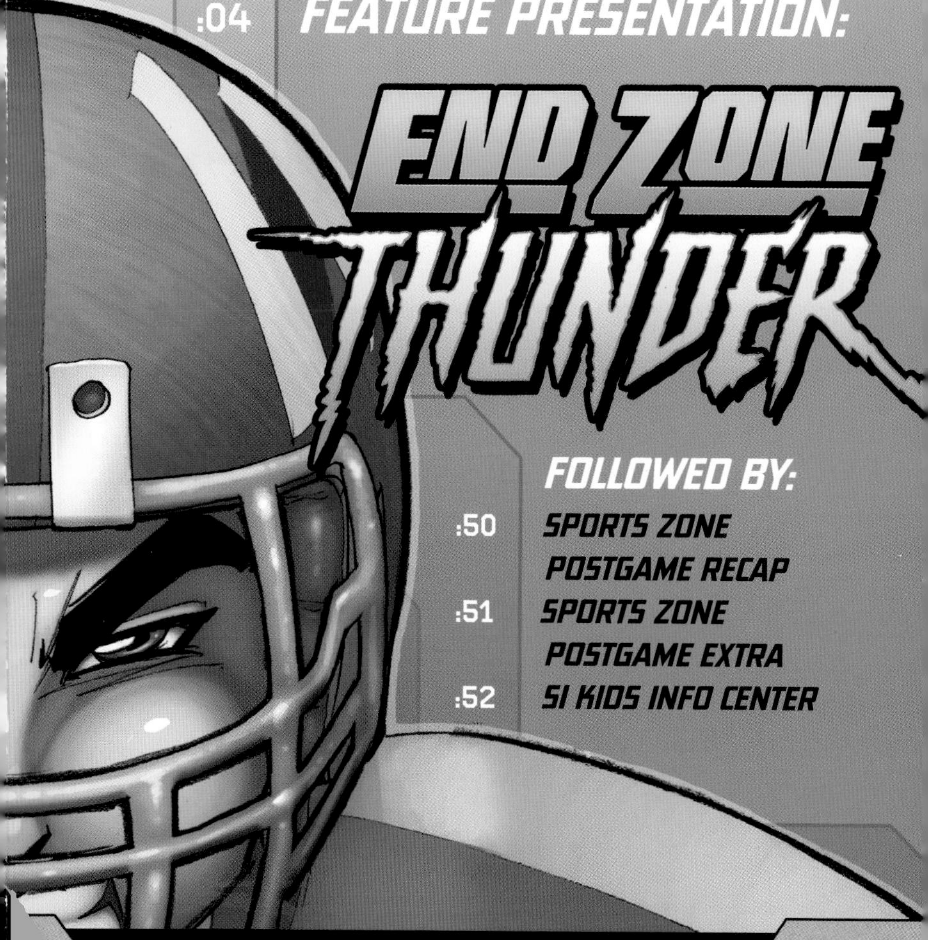

FOLLOWED BY:

:50 SPORTS ZONE POSTGAME RECAP

:51 SPORTS ZONE POSTGAME EXTRA

:52 SI KIDS INFO CENTER

TWO TALENTED WIDE RECEIVERS LEAD UNDEFEATED CYCLONES ATTACK   SIK TICKER

PORTS ZONE

ECIAL REPORT

"LIGHTNING" STRIKES AND "THUNDER" ROLLS, LEADING CYCLONES TO PERFECT RECORD

HANK WILDE

STATS:
NICKNAME: THUNDER
AGE: 14
POSITION: RECEIVER

BIO: Hank "Thunder" Wilde plays like he has something to prove, which makes sense, considering Jonas "Lightning" Fine is out to steal his thunder. These two talented wide receivers are both set to break team records, but there's only so many passes to go around. If they can't find a way to share the ball, the forecast for the Cyclone's post-season hopes is cloudy and bleak.

Sports Illustrated KIDS

UP NEXT: END ZONE THUNDER

BLZ vs
3-1
TGR vs
33:
EAG vs
14-7
SPA vs
4-3
BAN vs
21-1
RZR vs
4-3
BLZ vs
3-1

JONAS FINE

NICKNAME: LIGHTNING
AGE: 14 POSITION: RECEIVER

BIO: Jonas "Lightning" Fine is flashy and quick — a direct contrast to Hank Wilde's hard-nosed, straightforward playing style. The two make a great receiving core — that is, when they're not fighting over the ball...

TYREE BONAVENTURA

AGE: 14 POSITION: QUARTERBACK
BIO: Tyree is a talented quarterback who hopes to fill the shoes of team captain and starting QB, Craig Baldi.

BONAVENTURA

TOU YANG

AGE: 14 POSITION: UTILITY
BIO: Far and away the smallest player on the team, "Tiny Tou" hits like a truck. Despite his undersized frame, he plays a variety of positions.

YANG

CARLOS RAMIREZ

AGE: 14 POSITION: DEFENSIVE END
BIO: Carlos Ramirez has his sights set on opposing quarterbacks. His tackling skills are second-to-none.

RAMIREZ

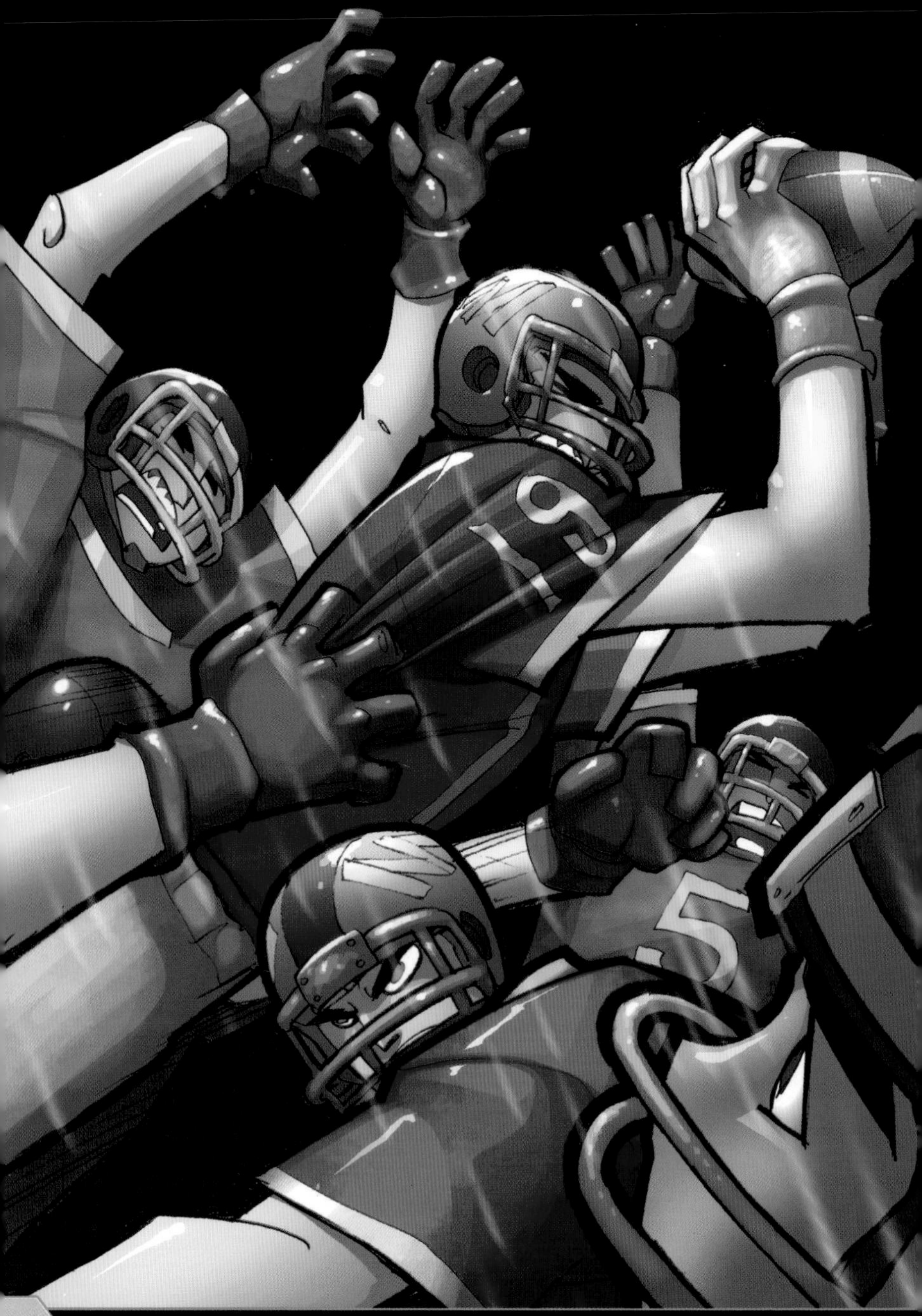

THE CYCLONES' TALENTED PASSING ATTACK AND SOLID DEFENSE GIVES T

PRESENTS

A PRODUCTION OF

STONE ARCH BOOKS
a capstone imprint

written by *Scott Ciencin*
illustrated by *Gerardo Sandoval*
colored by *Benny Fuentes*

designed and directed by *Bob Lentz*
edited by *Sean Tulien*
creative direction by *Heather Kindseth*
editorial direction by *Michael Dahl*

Sports Illustrated KIDS *End Zone Thunder* is published by Stone Arch Books,
A Capstone Imprint
1710 Roe Crest Drive, North Mankato, Minnesota 56003.
www.capstonepub.com

Summary: Hank "Thunder" Wilde and Jonas "Lightning" Fine are total
opposites. Jonas is flashy, while Hank lets his booming hits do the talking.
However, both teens have one thing in common — their competition
to become team captain is hurting the Cyclones' run at the state
championship. Will "Thunder" and "Lightning" rip the Cyclones apart, or
will the two wide receivers come together to create the perfect offensive
storm?

Cataloging-in-Publication Data is available at the Library of Congress
website.

ISBN 978-1-4342-2010-3 (library binding)
ISBN 978-1-4342-2784-3 (paperback)
ISBN 978-1-4342-4942-5 (e-book pdf)

Printed and bound in China. PO4842

WELL-ROUNDED TEAM CAPABLE OF GOING FAR IN THE PLAYOFFS   SIK TICKER

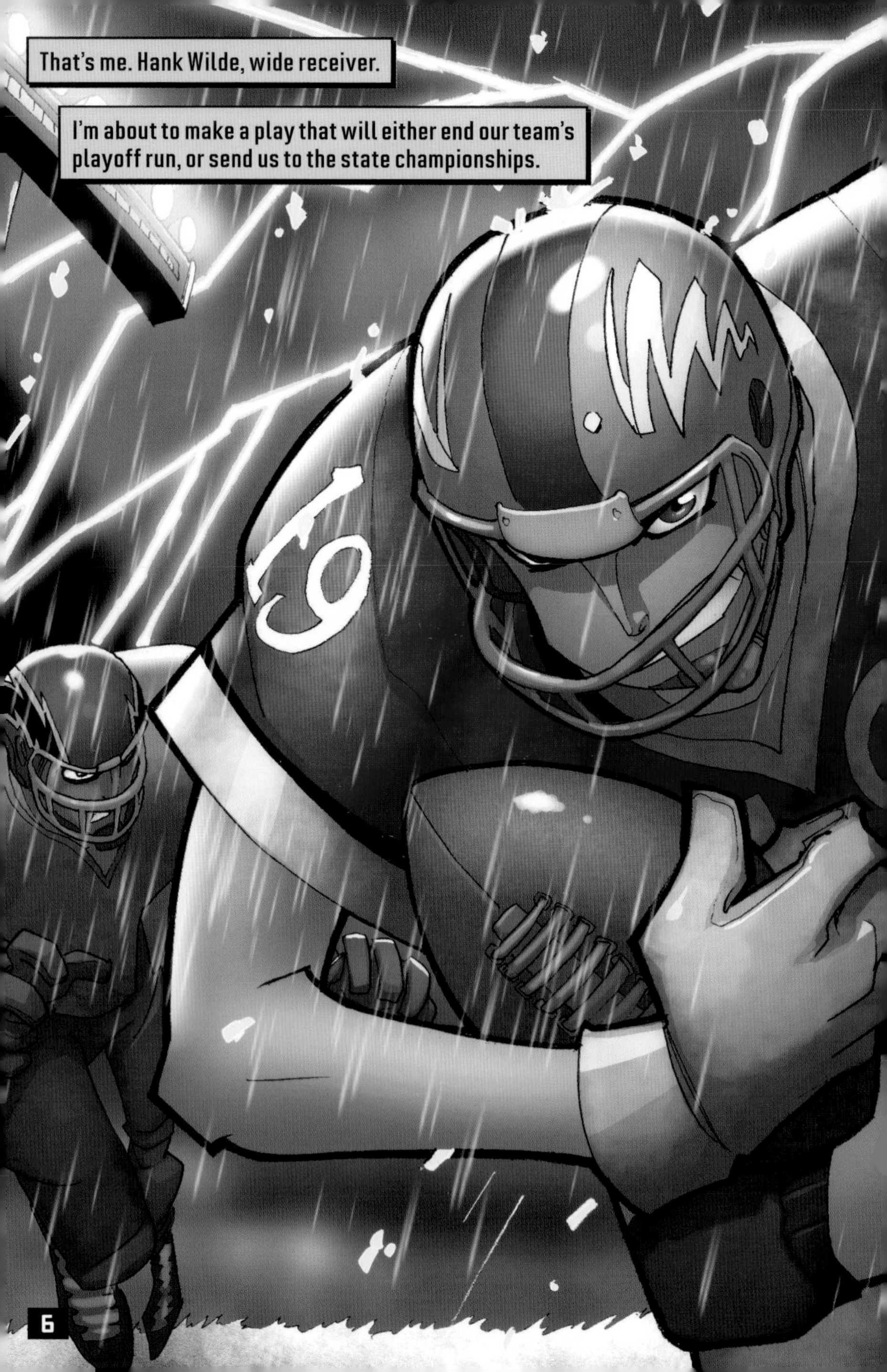
That's me. Hank Wilde, wide receiver.
I'm about to make a play that will either end our team's playoff run, or send us to the state championships.

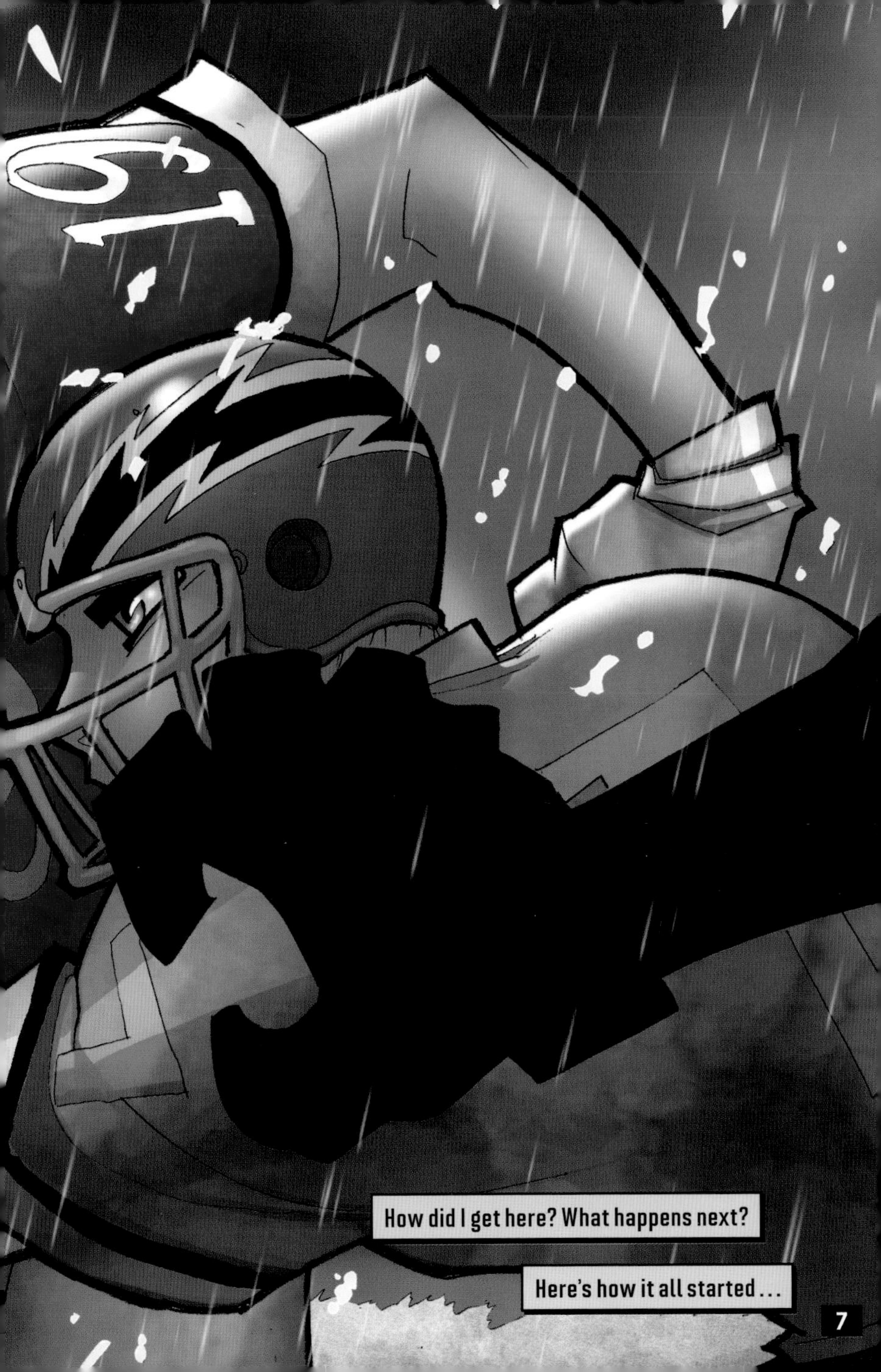
How did I get here? What happens next?
Here's how it all started . . .

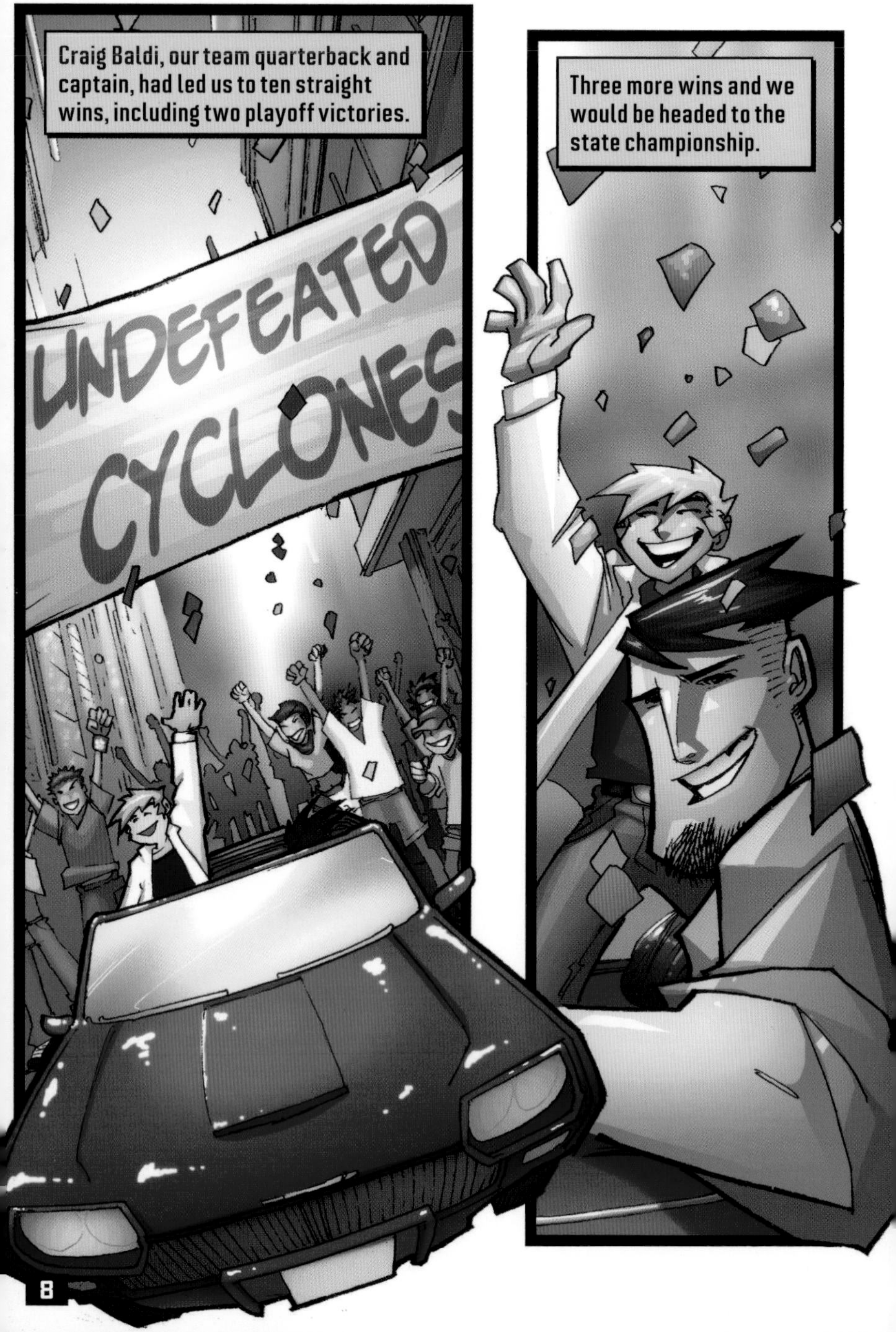
Craig Baldi, our team quarterback and captain, had led us to ten straight wins, including two playoff victories.
UNDEFEATED CYCLONES
Three more wins and we would be headed to the state championship.

Then Craig dropped a bomb on us.

My dad got a job in Los Angeles. We're moving this weekend.

This will be my last game with the Cyclones . . . so, help me go out on a win!

The Somerset Hawks never knew what hit them.

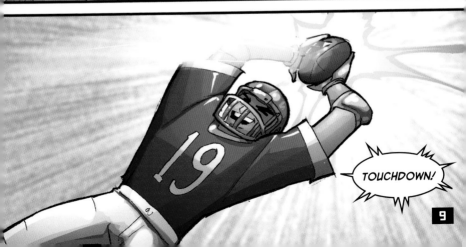

TOUCHDOWN!

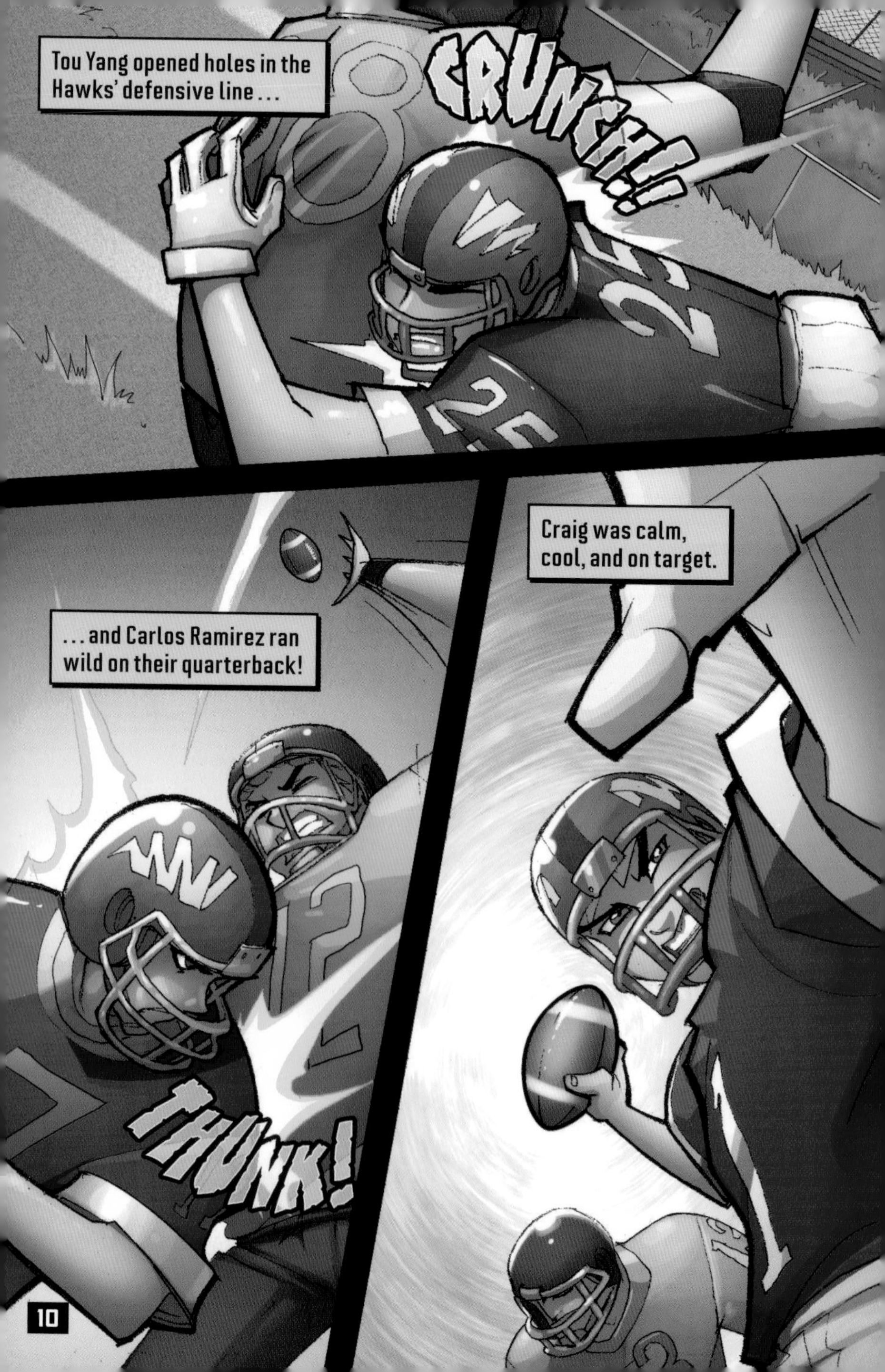
Tou Yang opened holes in the Hawks' defensive line . . .
CRUNCH!!!
. . . and Carlos Ramirez ran wild on their quarterback!
THUNK!
Craig was calm, cool, and on target.

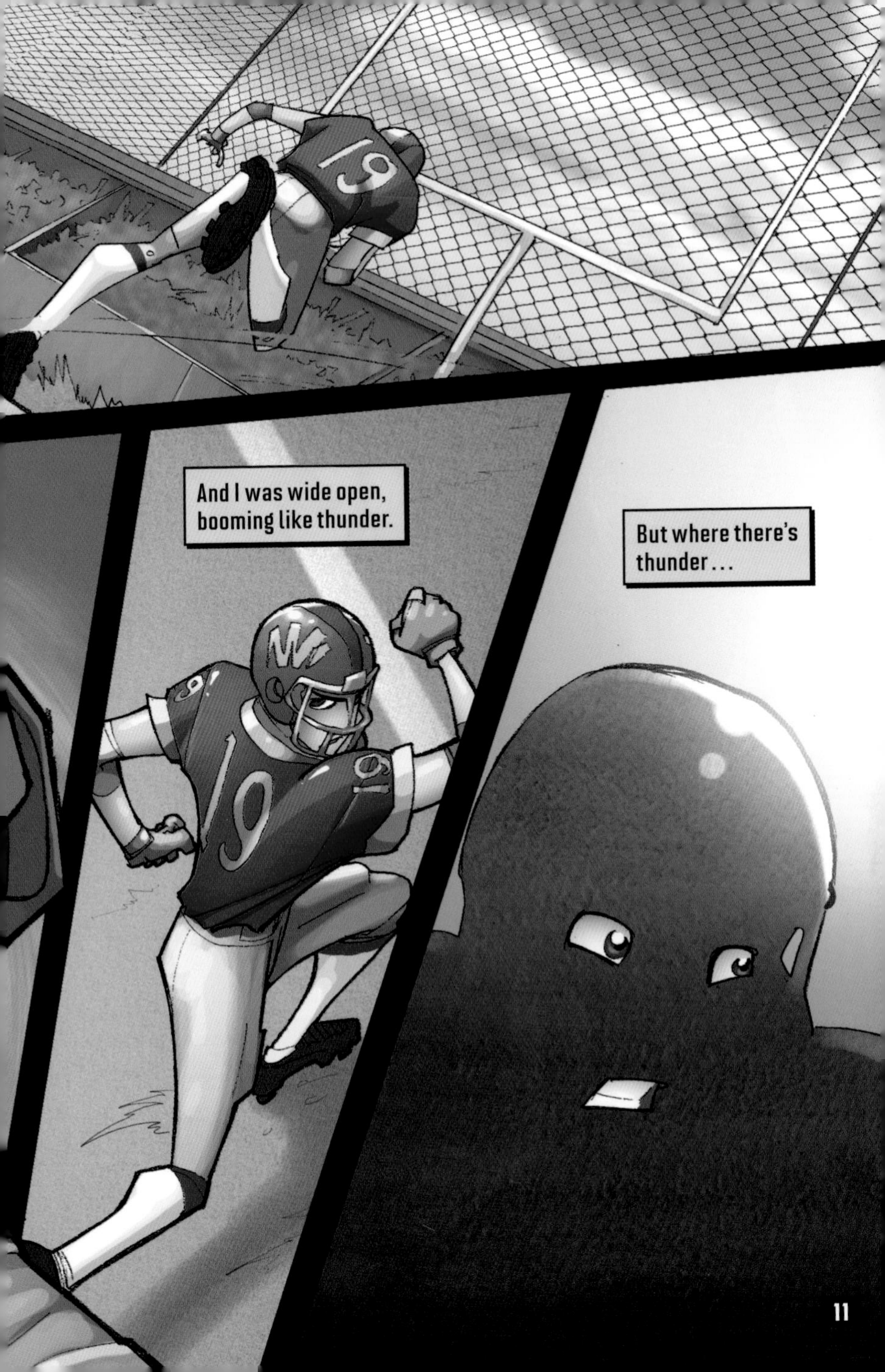
And I was wide open, booming like thunder.
But where there's thunder . . .

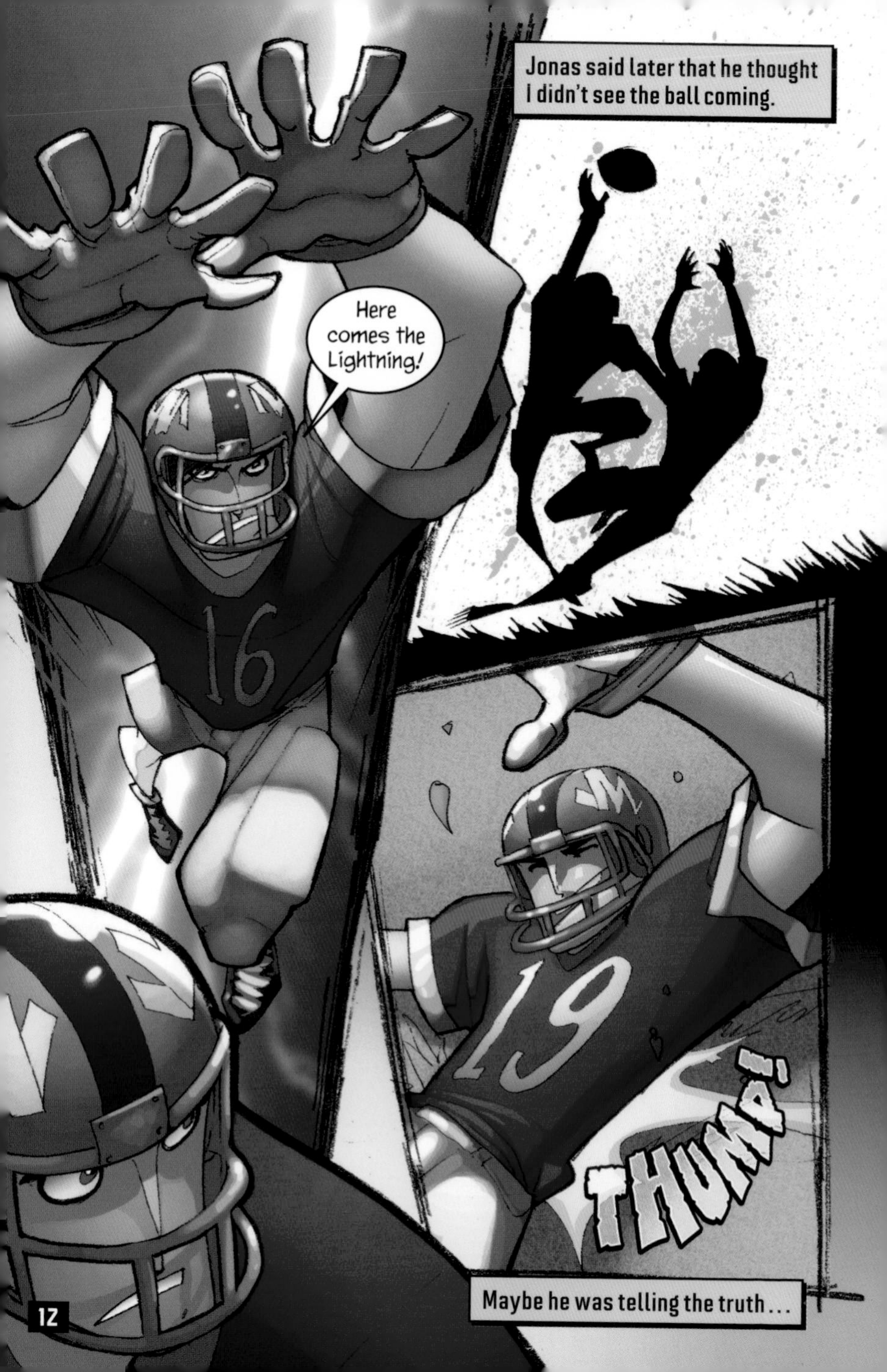
Jonas said later that he thought I didn't see the ball coming.
Here comes the Lightning!
THUMP!
Maybe he was telling the truth...

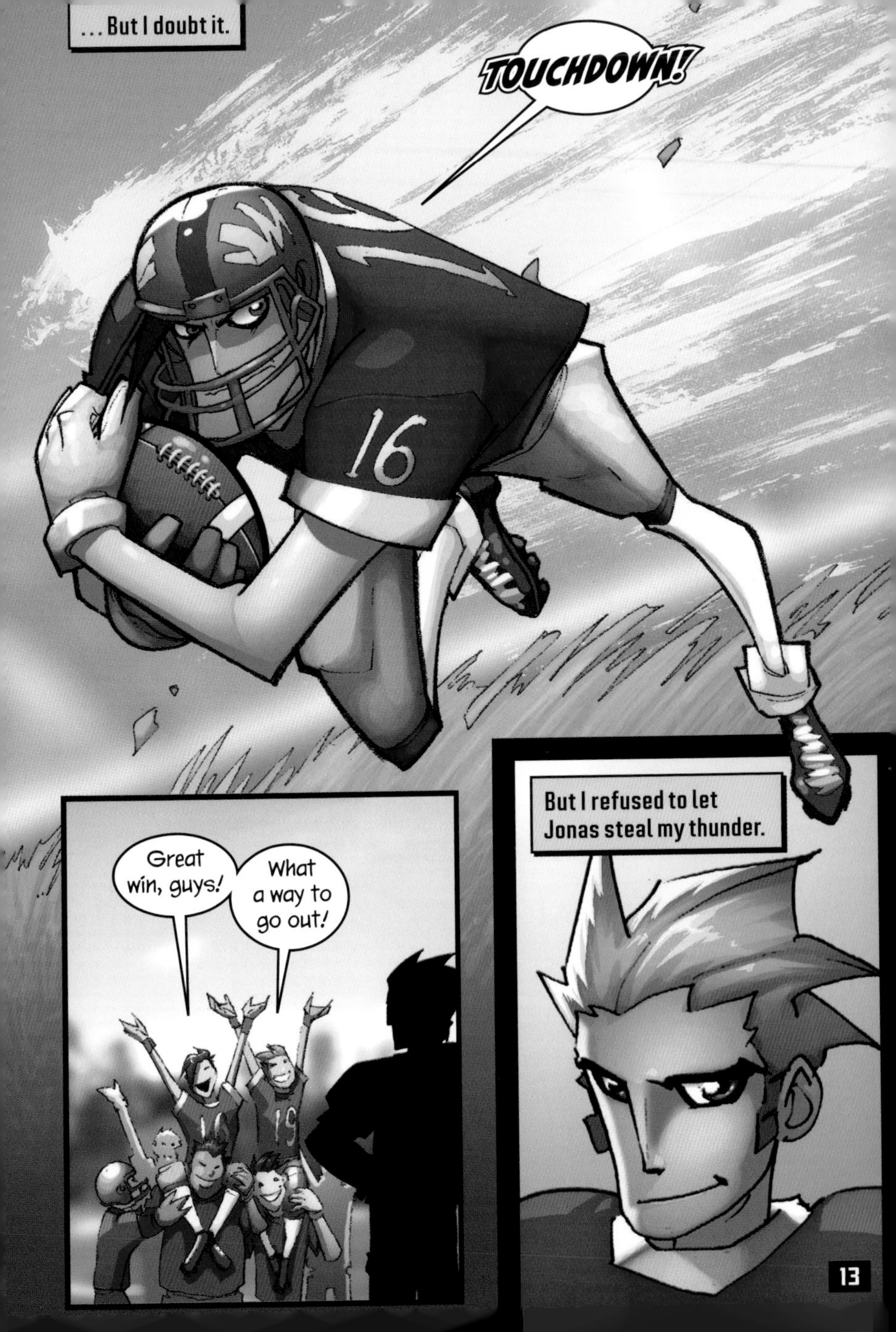

...But I doubt it.
TOUCHDOWN!
16
Great win, guys!
What a way to go out!
19
But I refused to let Jonas steal my thunder.

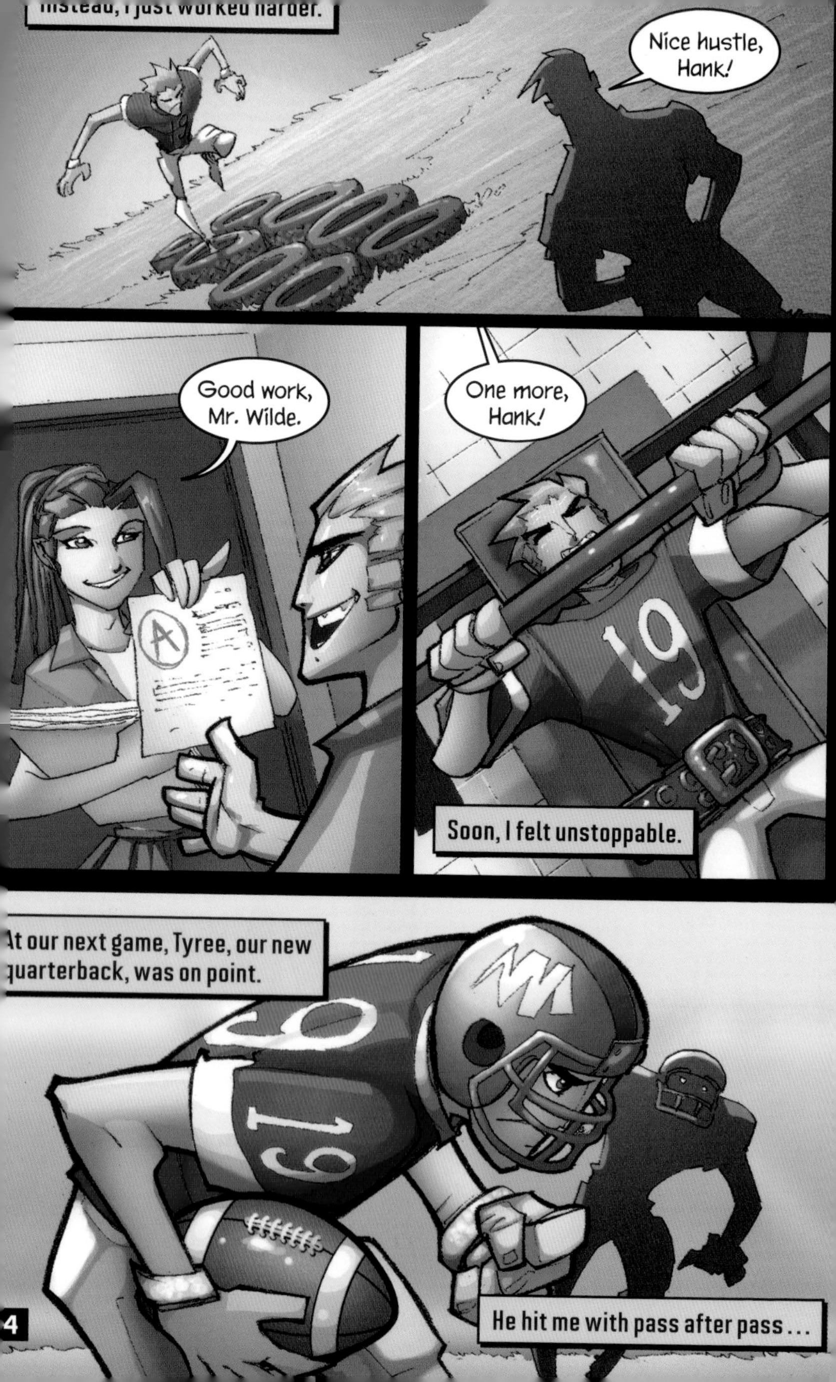
Instead, I just worked harder.
Nice hustle, Hank!
Good work, Mr. Wilde.
One more, Hank!
Soon, I felt unstoppable.
At our next game, Tyree, our new quarterback, was on point.
He hit me with pass after pass . . .

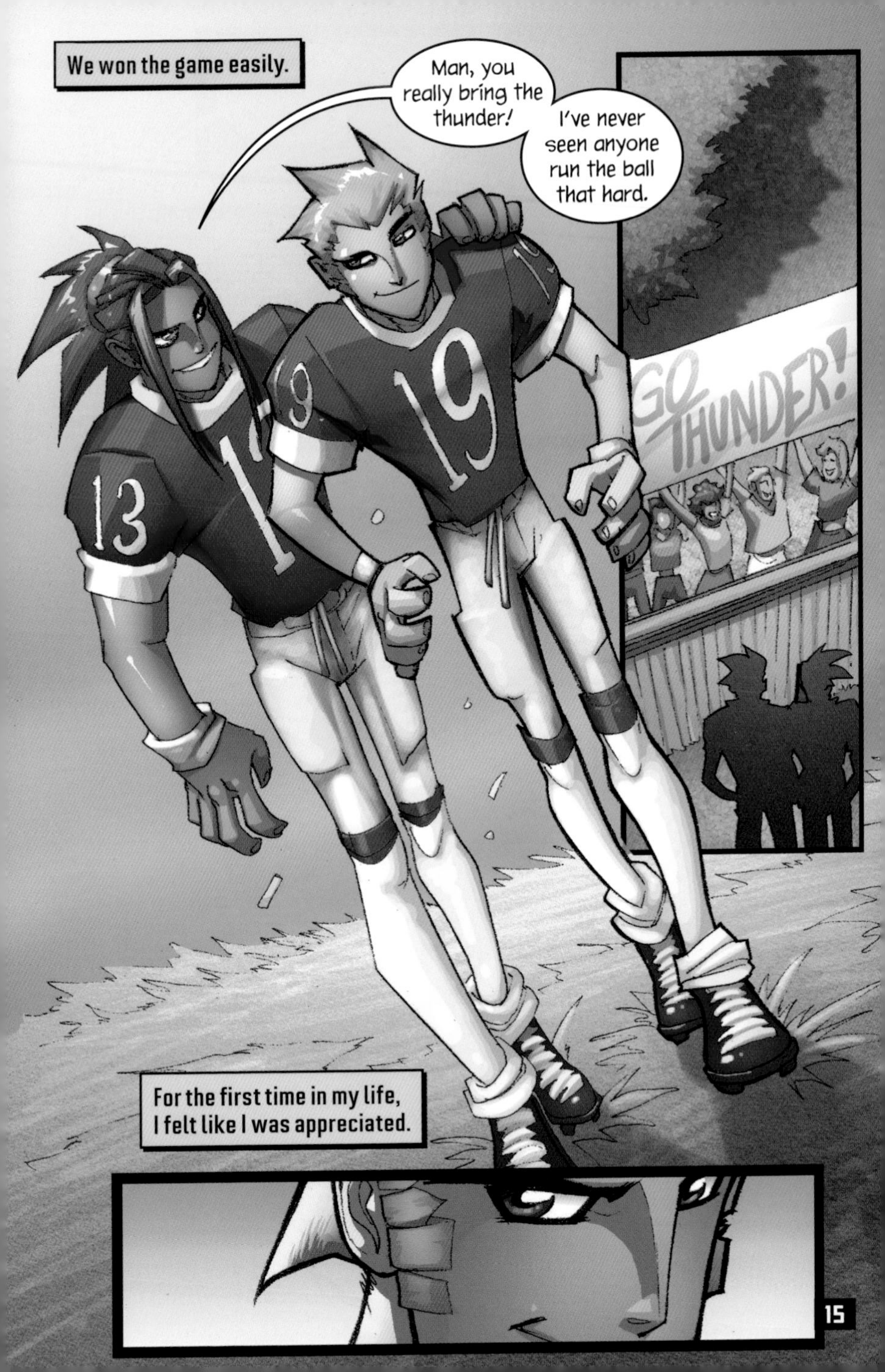
We won the game easily.
Man, you really bring the thunder!
I've never seen anyone run the ball that hard.
GO THUNDER!
13
19
19
For the first time in my life, I felt like I was appreciated.

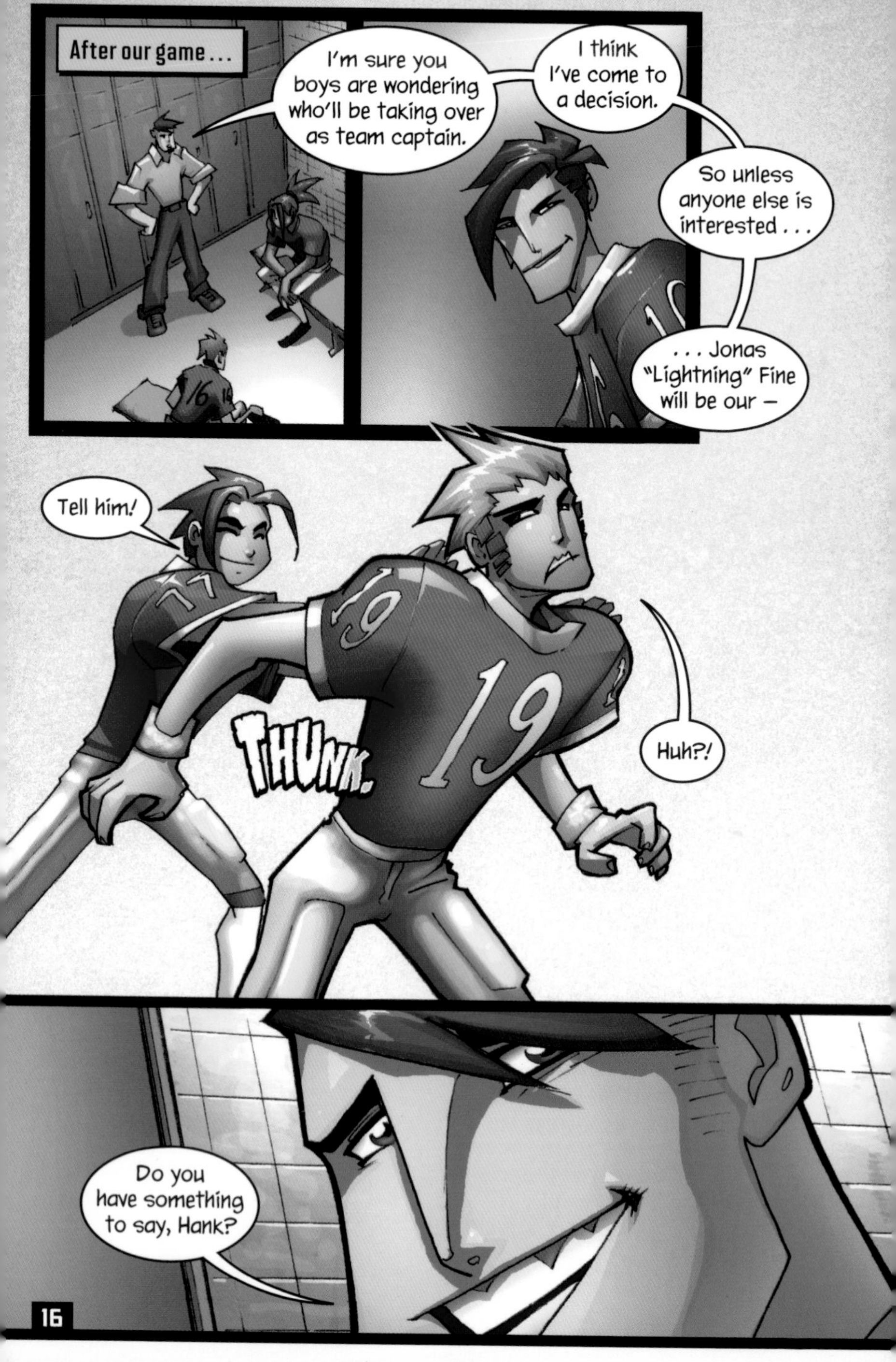
After our game . . .
I'm sure you boys are wondering who'll be taking over as team captain.
I think I've come to a decision.
So unless anyone else is interested . . .
. . . Jonas "Lightning" Fine will be our —
Tell him!
THUNK.
Huh?!
Do you have something to say, Hank?

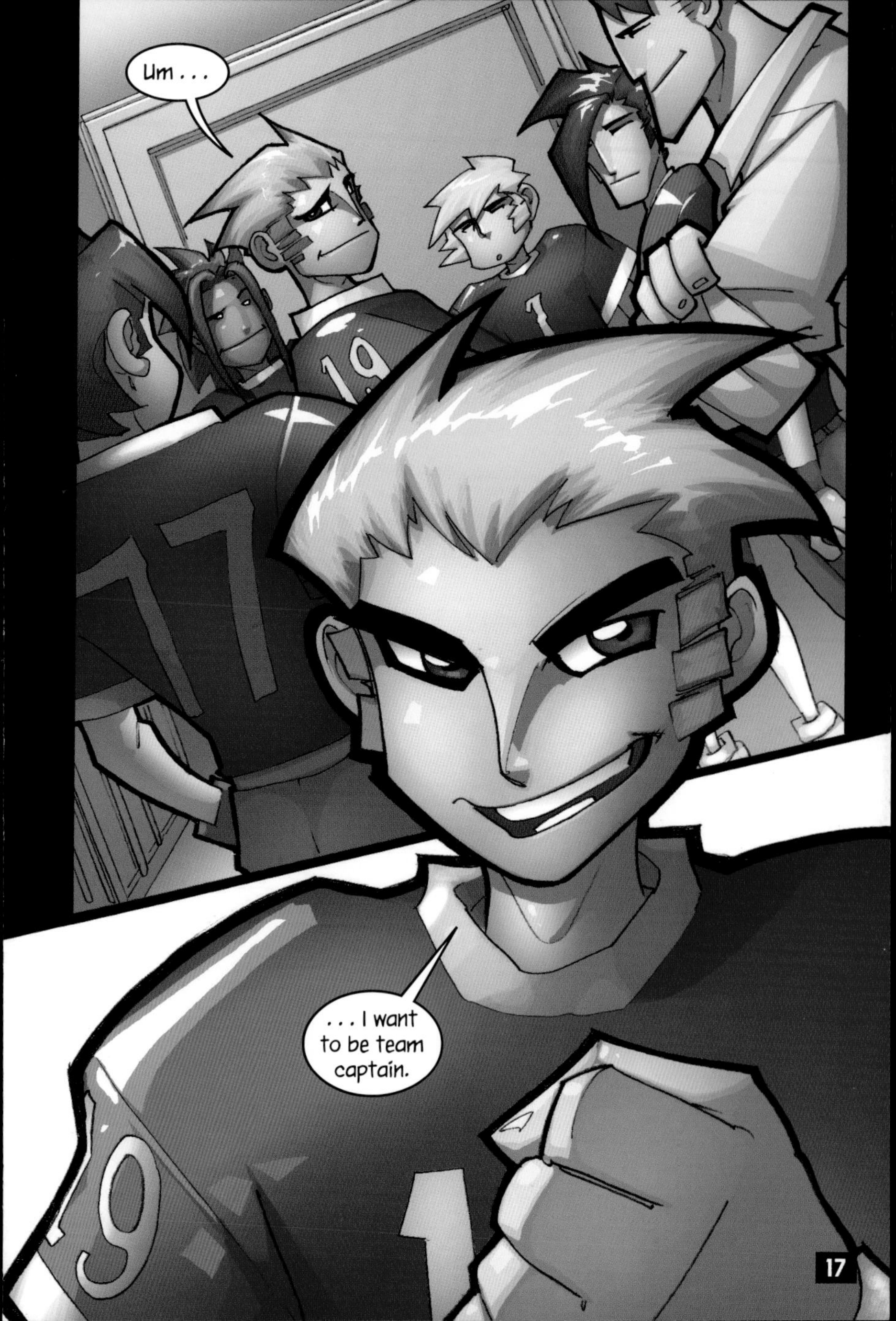
Um . . .
. . . I want to be team captain.

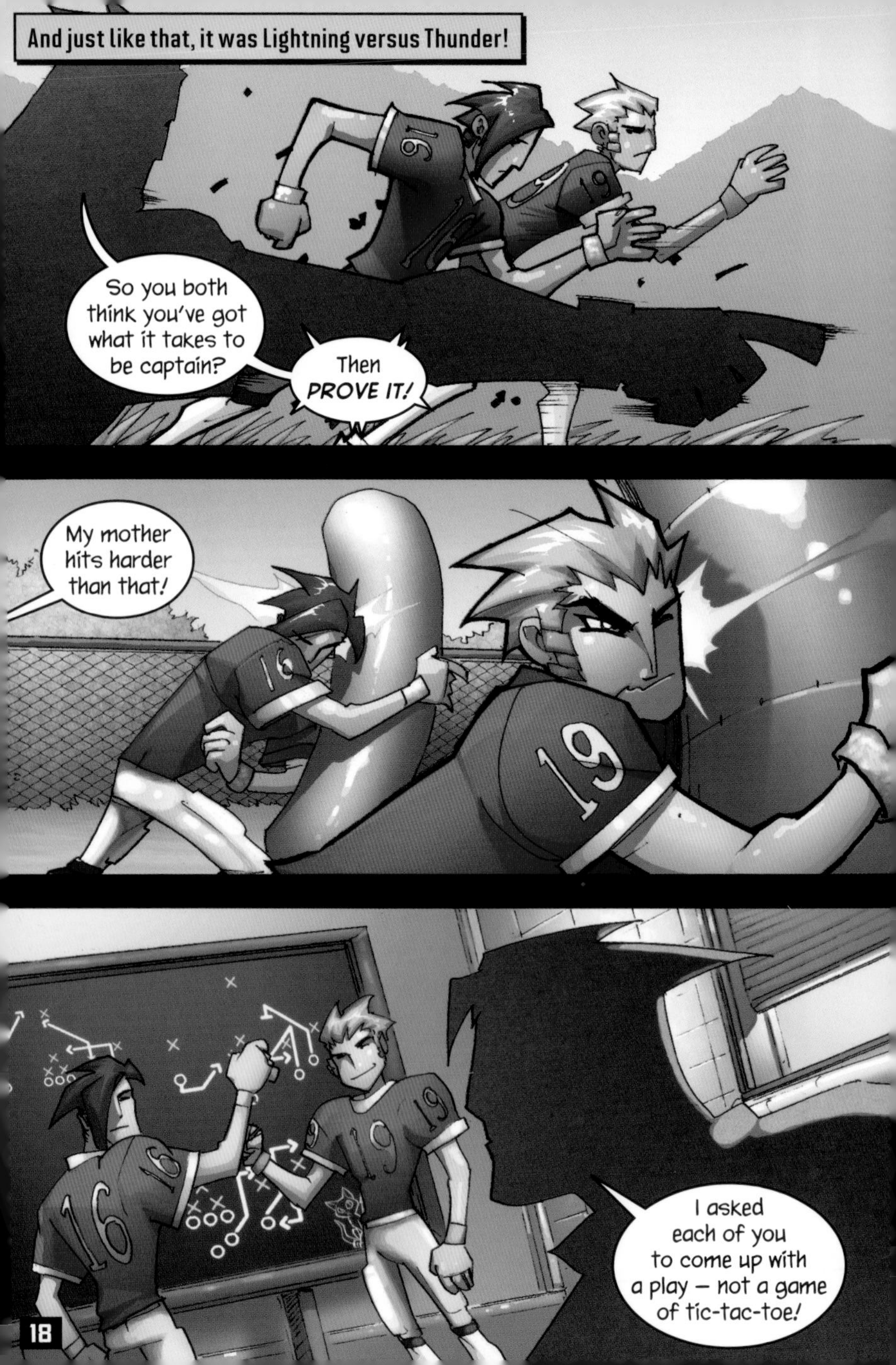

And just like that, it was Lightning versus Thunder!
So you both think you've got what it takes to be captain?
Then PROVE IT!
My mother hits harder than that!
I asked each of you to come up with a play — not a game of tic-tac-toe!

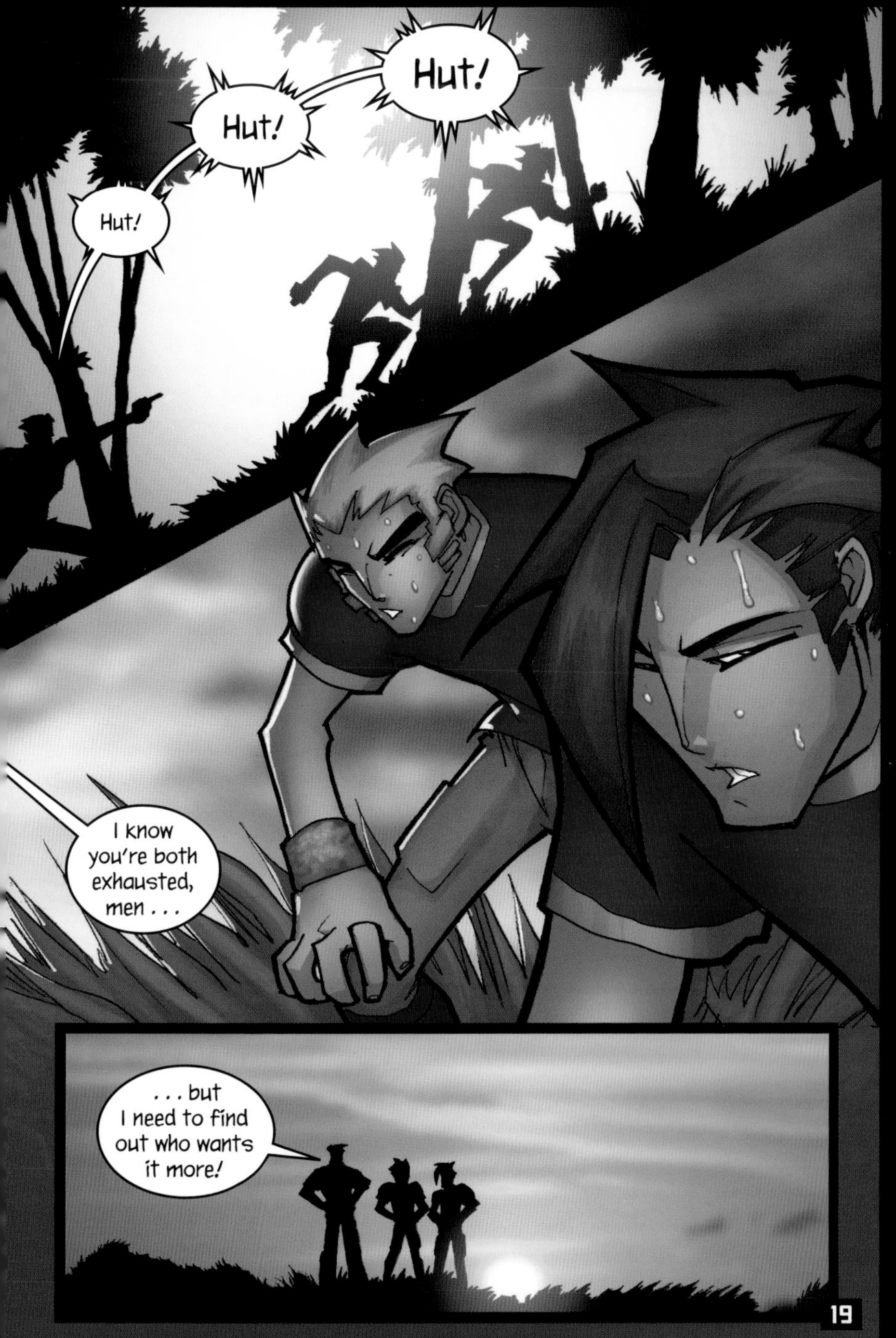
Hut!
Hut!
Hut!
I know you're both exhausted, men . . .
. . . but I need to find out who wants it more!

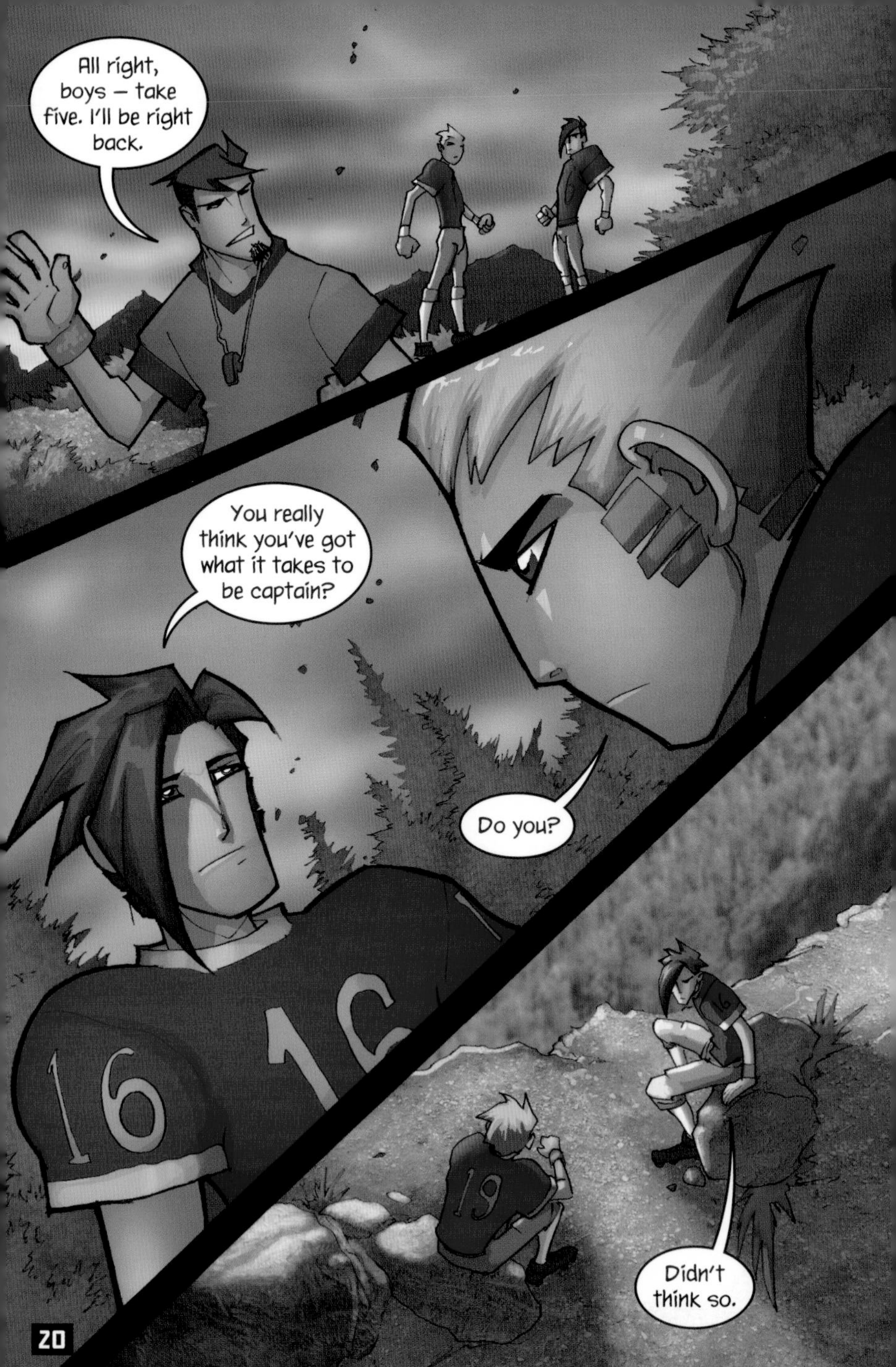
All right, boys — take five. I'll be right back.
You really think you've got what it takes to be captain?
Do you?
Didn't think so.

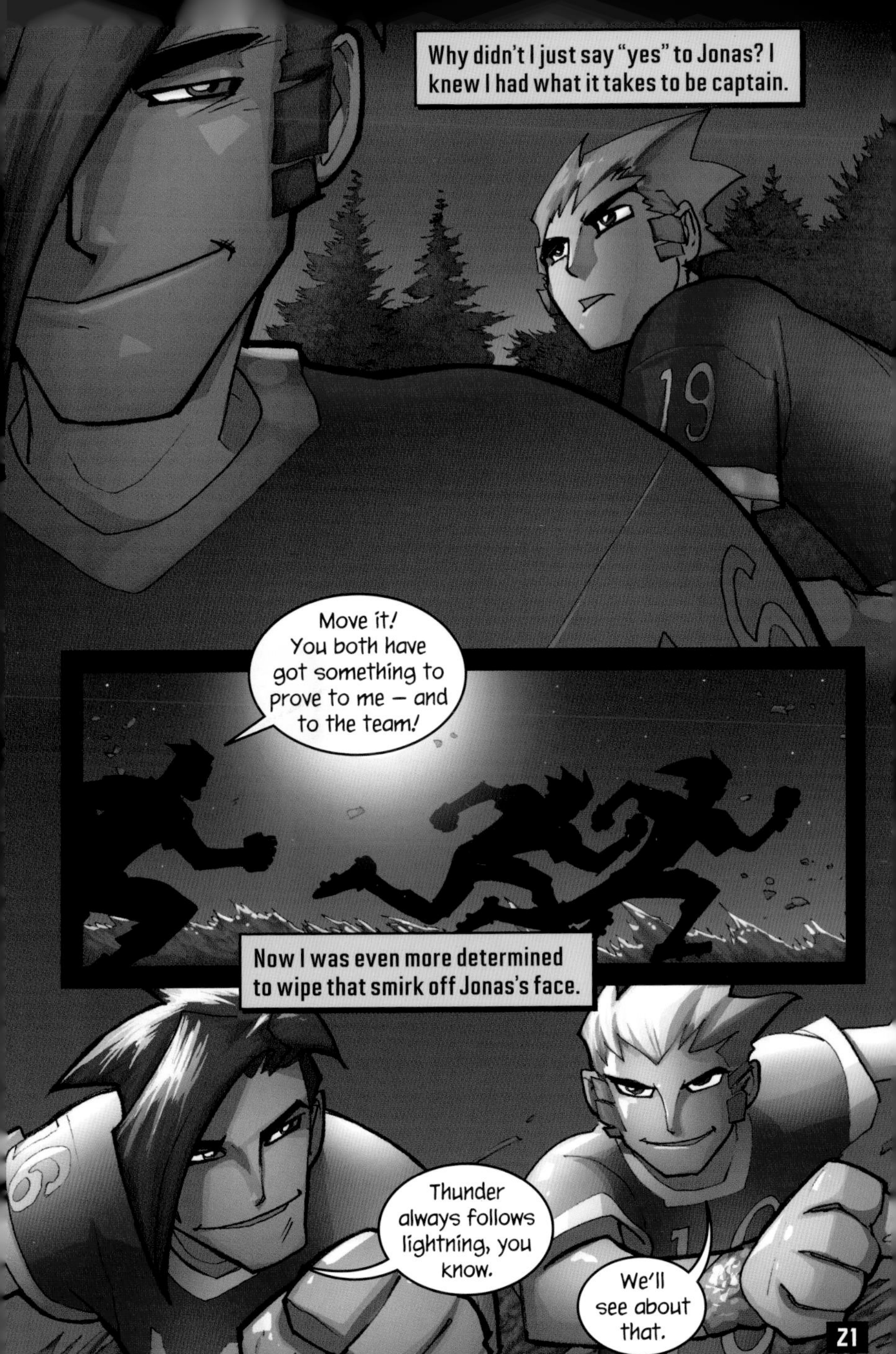
Why didn't I just say "yes" to Jonas? I knew I had what it takes to be captain.
19
Move it! You both have got something to prove to me — and to the team!
Now I was even more determined to wipe that smirk off Jonas's face.
Thunder always follows lightning, you know.
We'll see about that.

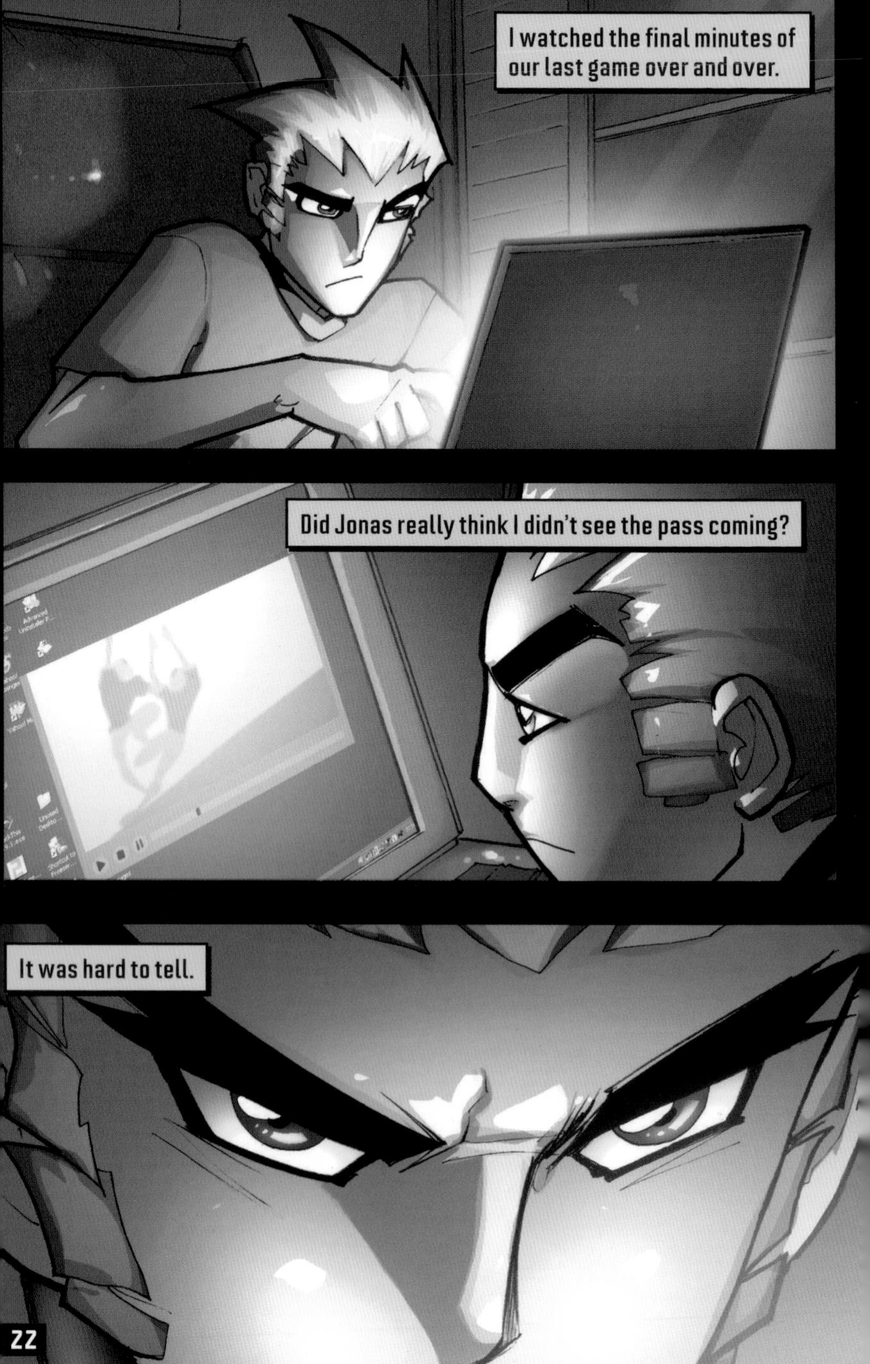
I watched the final minutes of our last game over and over.
Did Jonas really think I didn't see the pass coming?
It was hard to tell.

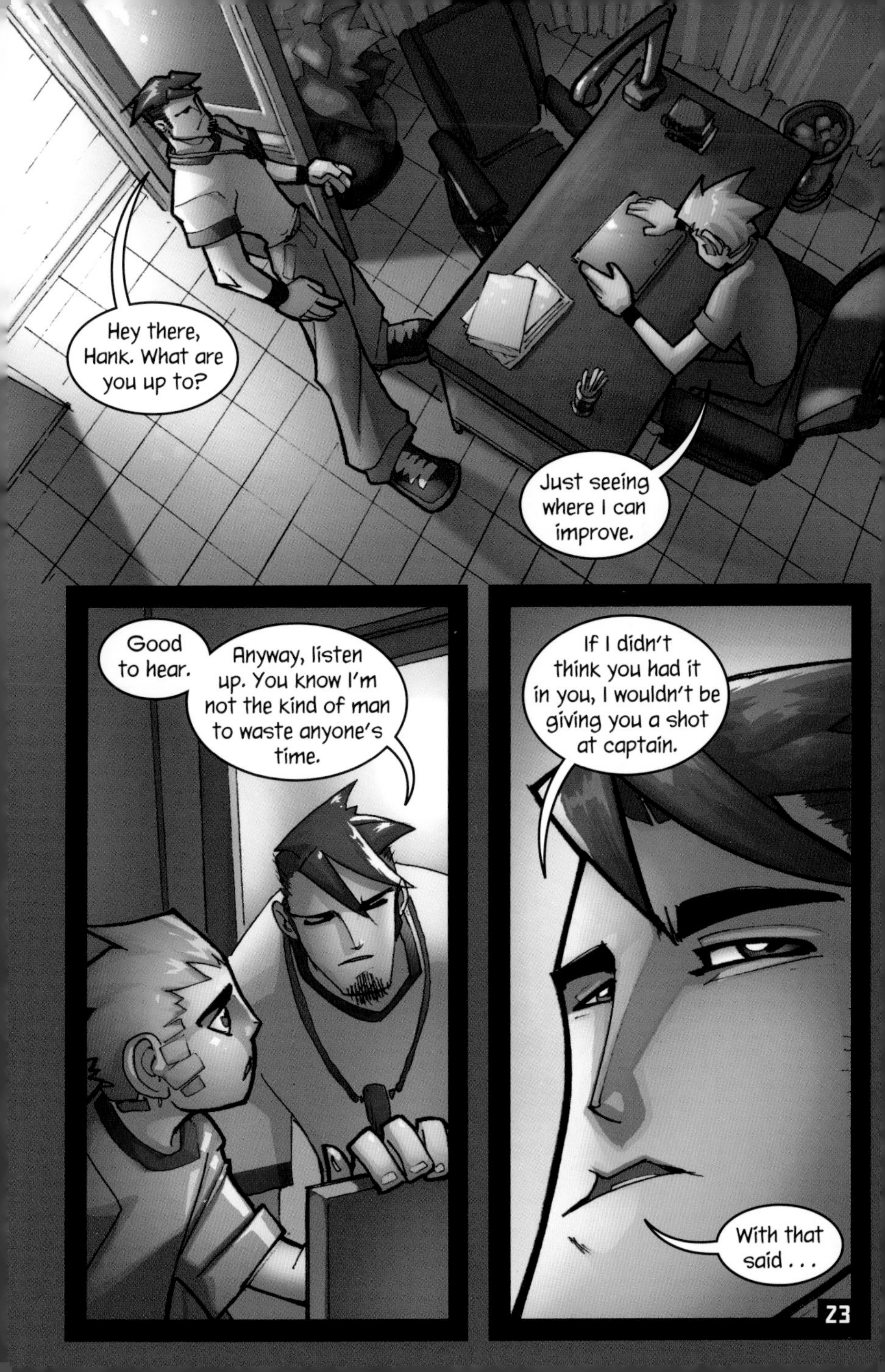

Hey there, Hank. What are you up to?
Just seeing where I can improve.
Good to hear.
Anyway, listen up. You know I'm not the kind of man to waste anyone's time.
If I didn't think you had it in you, I wouldn't be giving you a shot at captain.
With that said . . .

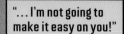
"...I'm not going to make it easy on you!"

So I've chosen two new ones!

You know, men, I don't think those tackling dummies are getting the job done anymore.

It was a long practice!

CRUNCH!

SMASH!

Moving kind of slow there, Hank.

Coach has really been pushing me.

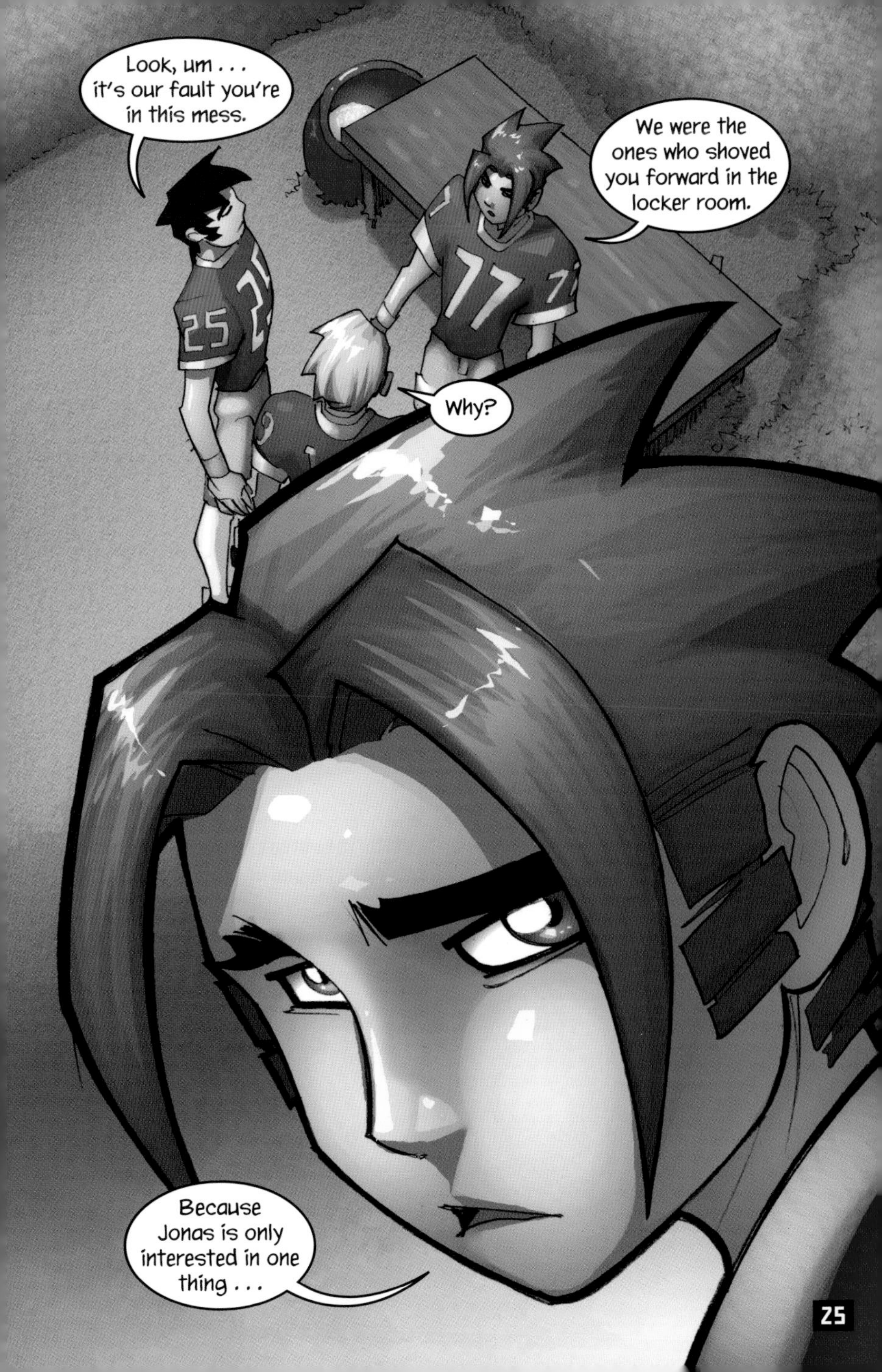
Look, um . . . it's our fault you're in this mess.
We were the ones who shoved you forward in the locker room.
Why?
Because Jonas is only interested in one thing . . .

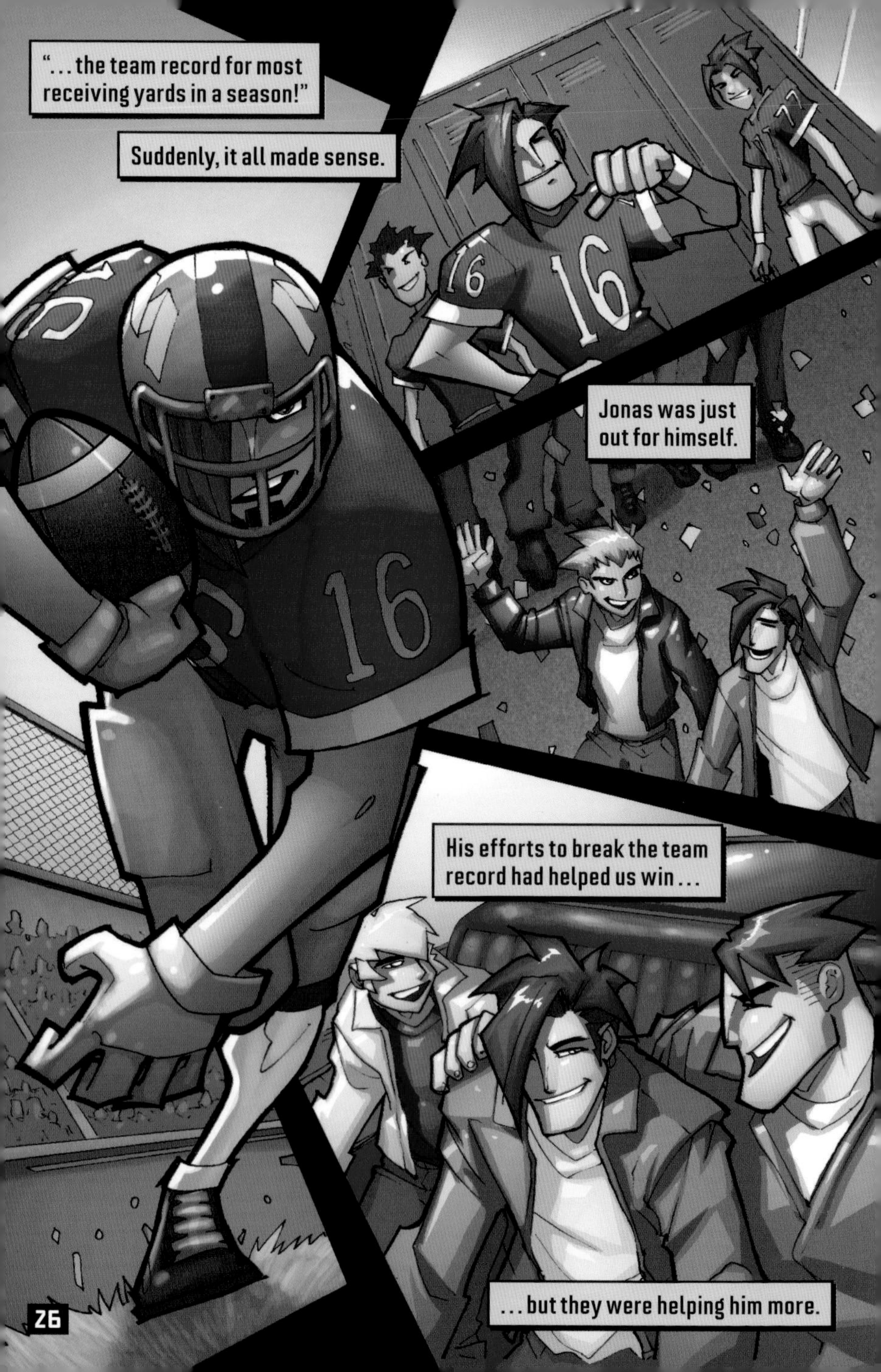
"... the team record for most receiving yards in a season!"
Suddenly, it all made sense.
Jonas was just out for himself.
His efforts to break the team record had helped us win ...
... but they were helping him more.

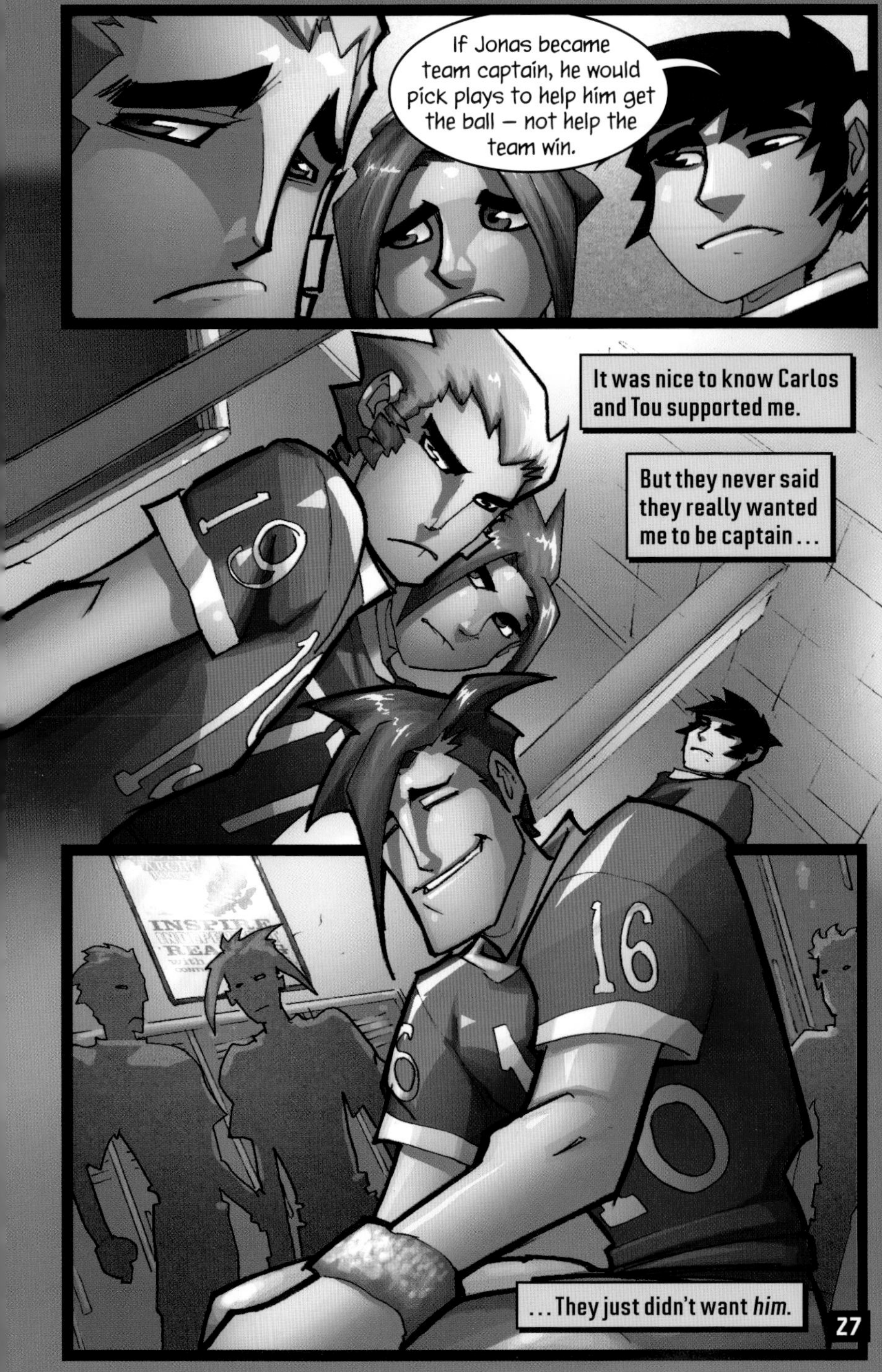
If Jonas became team captain, he would pick plays to help him get the ball — not help the team win.
It was nice to know Carlos and Tou supported me.
But they never said they really wanted me to be captain . . .
16
INSPIRE
. . . They just didn't want *him*.

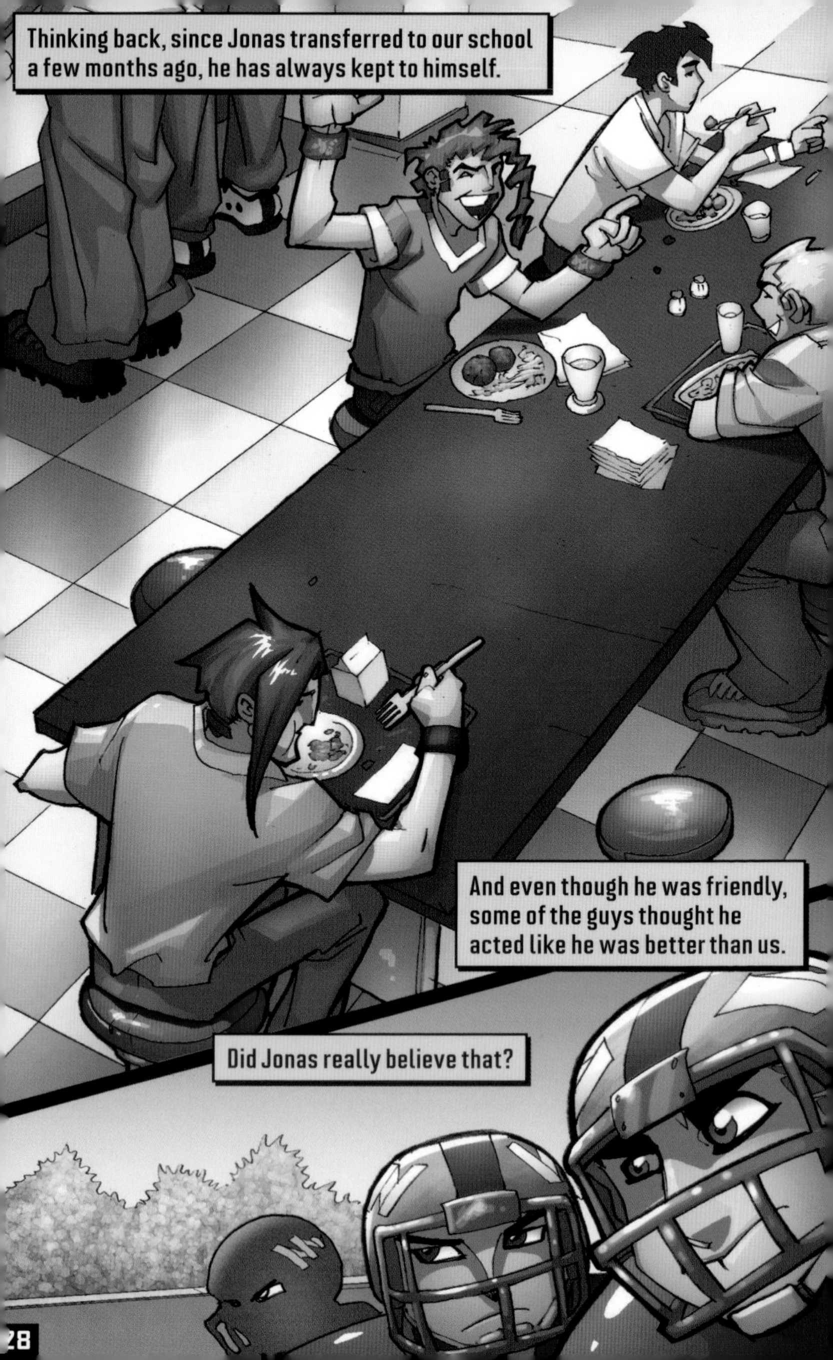
Thinking back, since Jonas transferred to our school a few months ago, he has always kept to himself.
And even though he was friendly, some of the guys thought he acted like he was better than us.
Did Jonas really believe that?

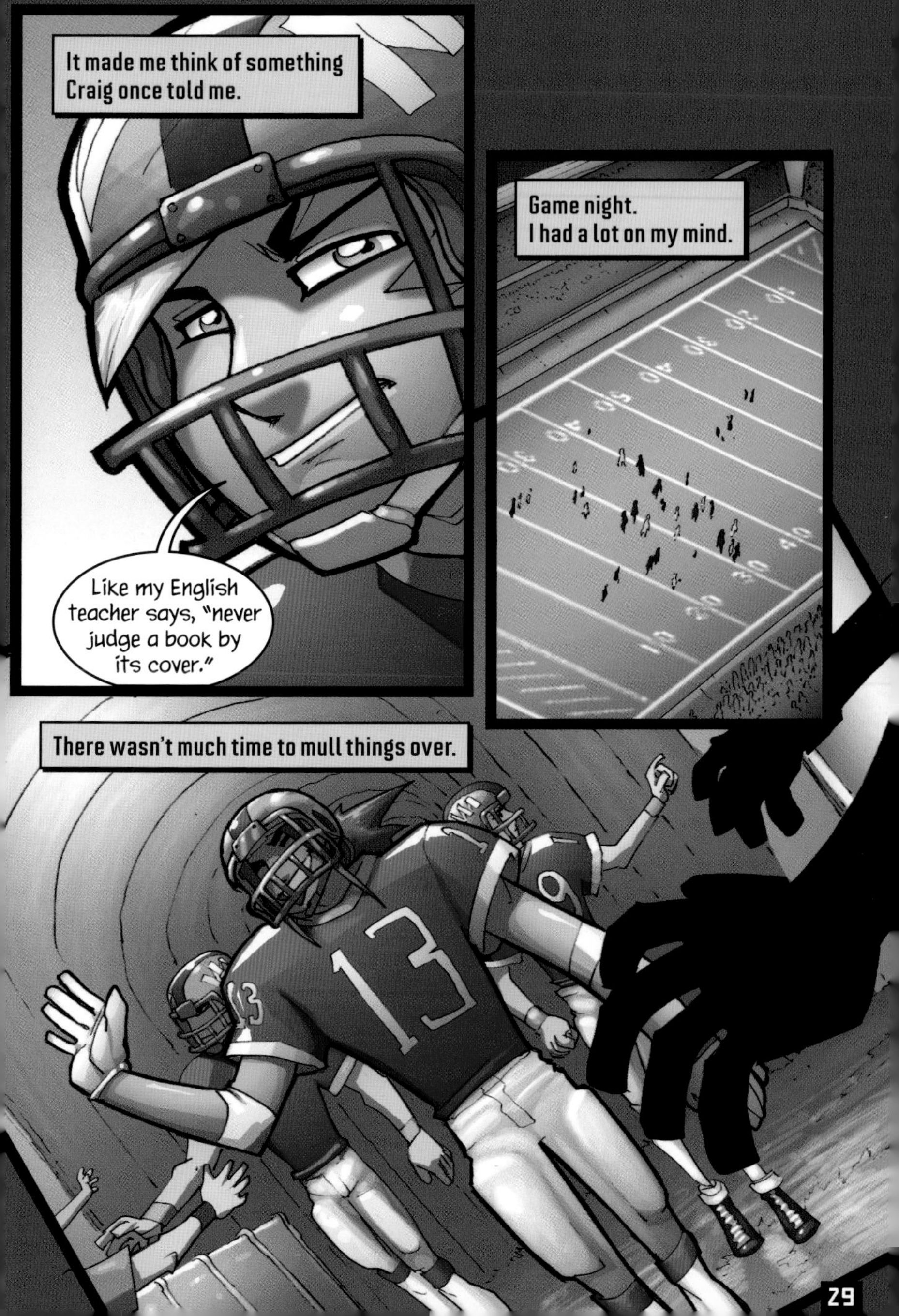
It made me think of something Craig once told me.
Like my English teacher says, "never judge a book by its cover."
Game night. I had a lot on my mind.
There wasn't much time to mull things over.

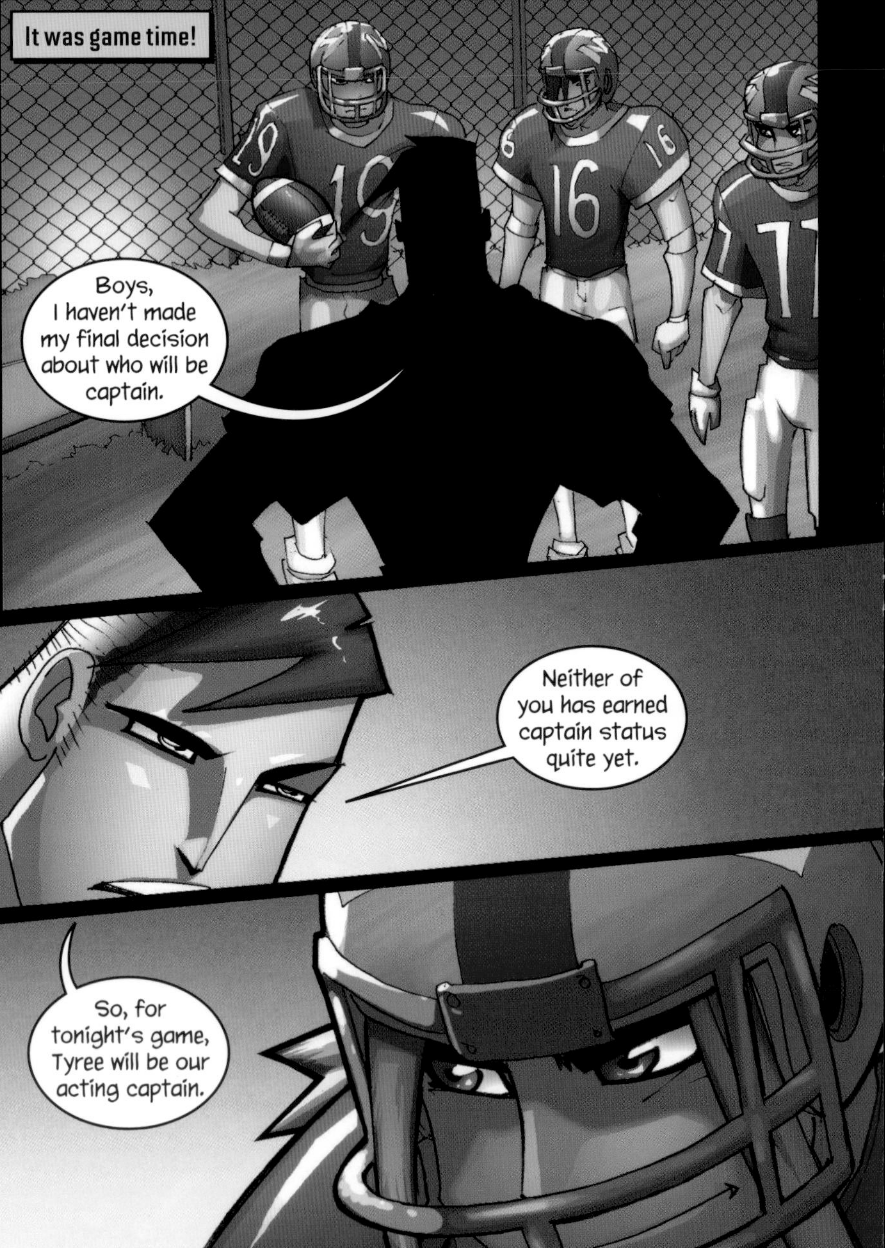
It was game time!
Boys, I haven't made my final decision about who will be captain.
Neither of you has earned captain status quite yet.
So, for tonight's game, Tyree will be our acting captain.

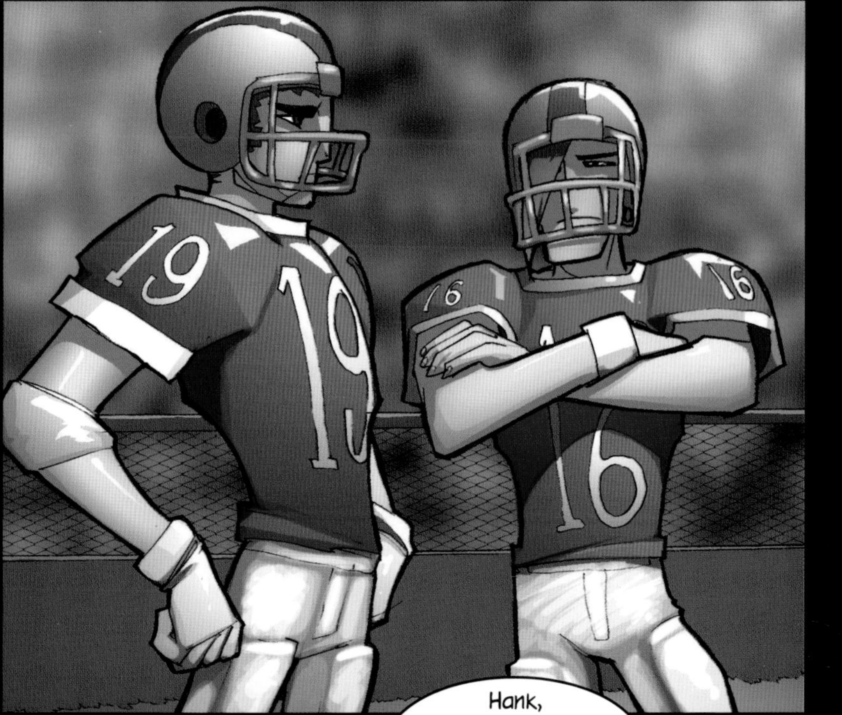

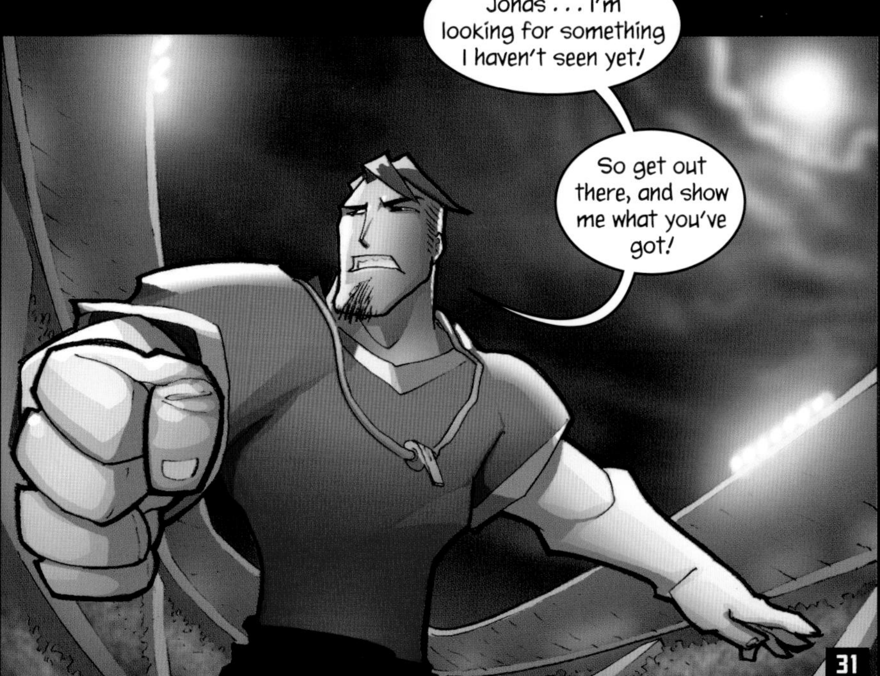
Hank, Jonas . . . I'm looking for something I haven't seen yet!
So get out there, and show me what you've got!

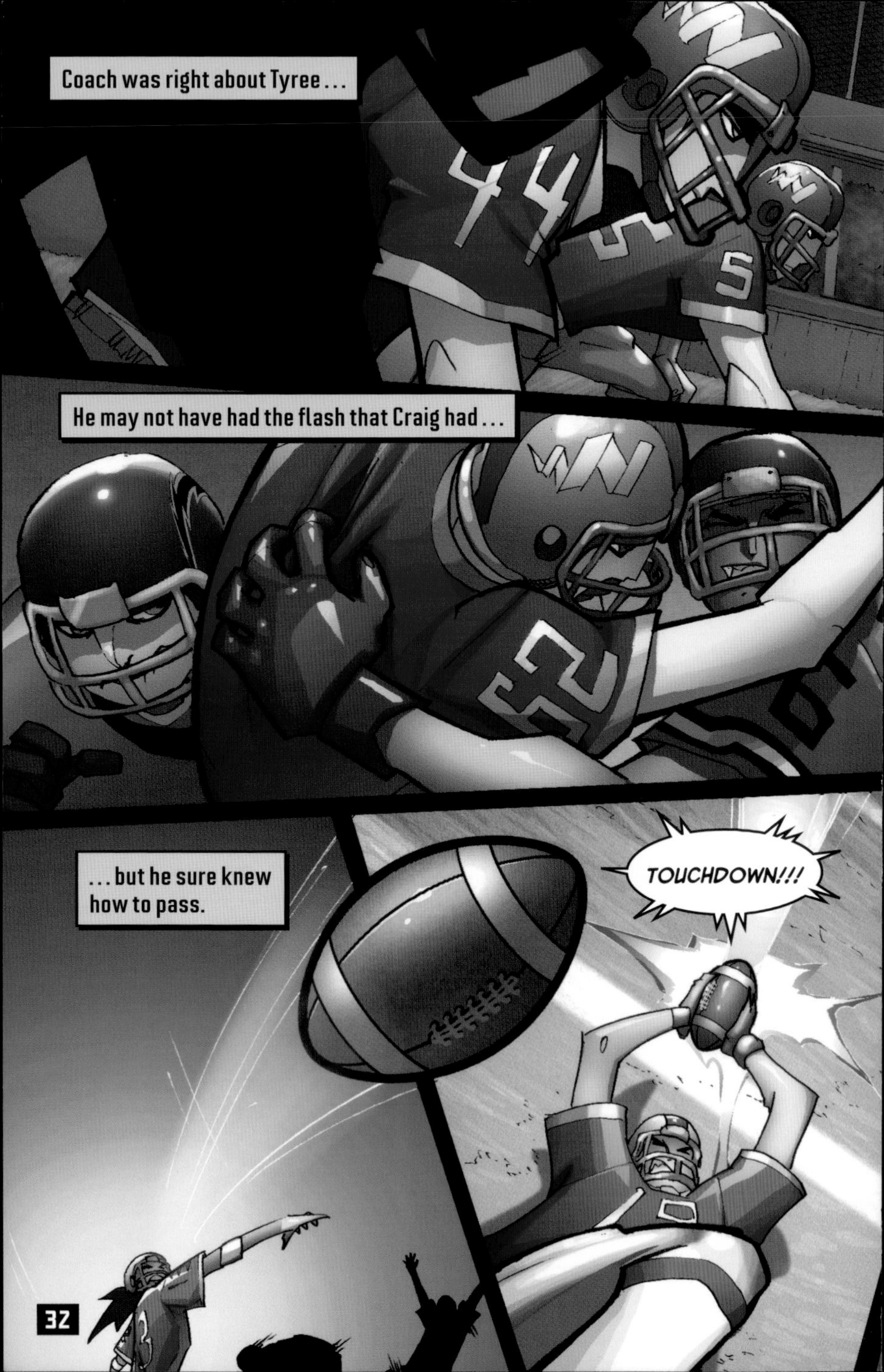
Coach was right about Tyree . . .
He may not have had the flash that Craig had . . .
. . . but he sure knew how to pass.
TOUCHDOWN!!!

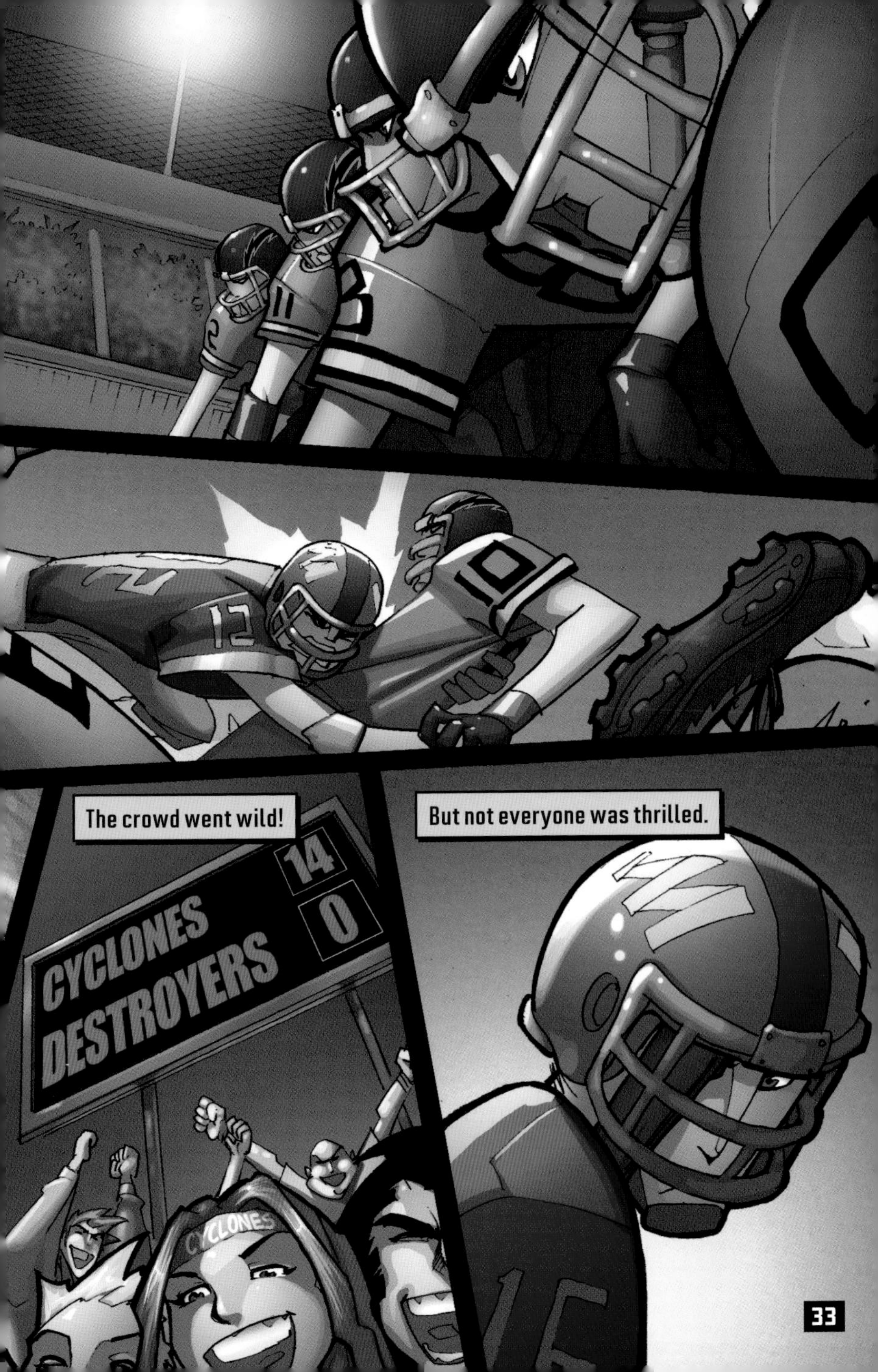
The crowd went wild!
CYCLONES
DESTROYERS
14
0
CYCLONES
But not everyone was thrilled.

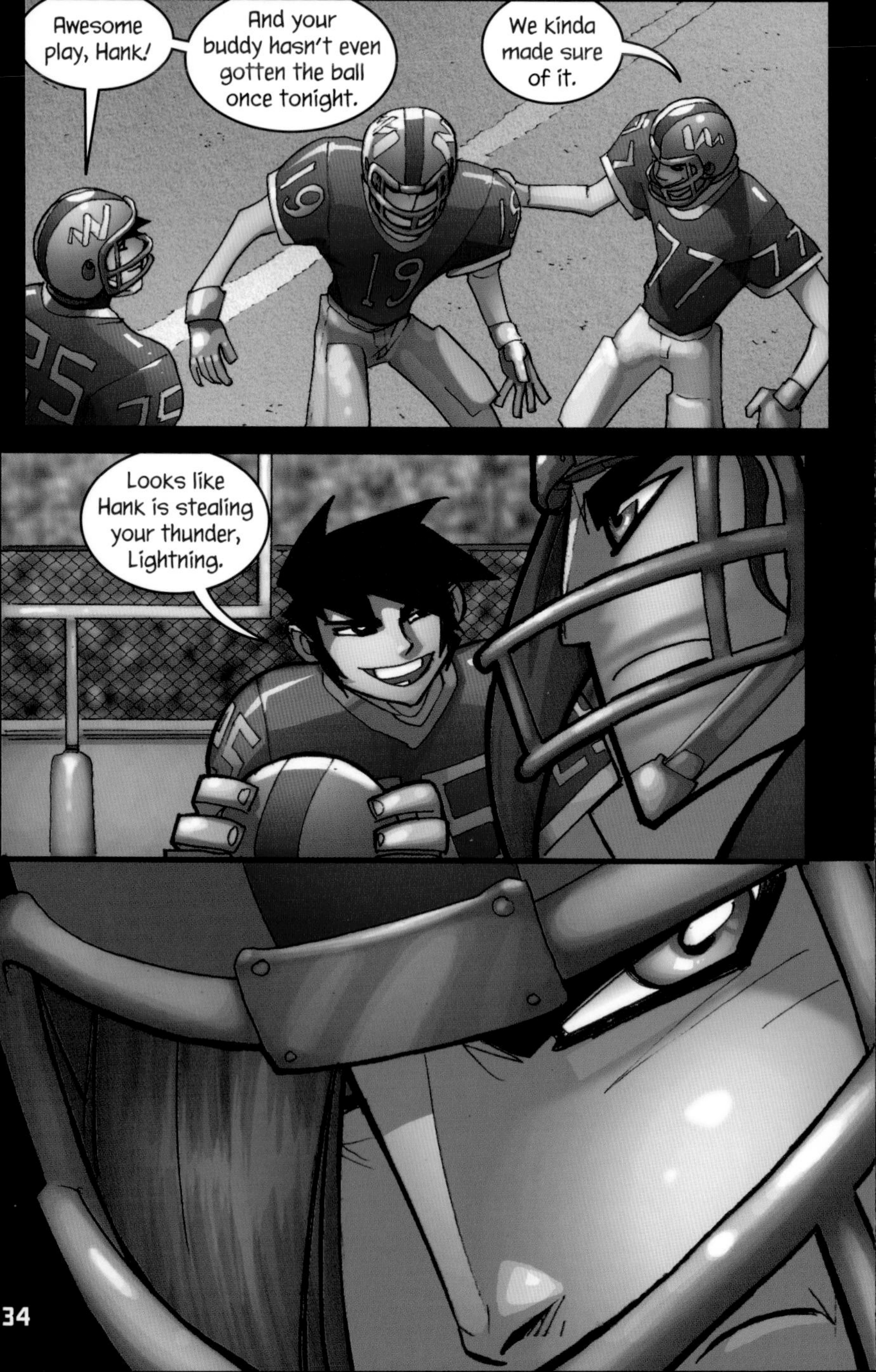
Awesome play, Hank!
And your buddy hasn't even gotten the ball once tonight.
We kinda made sure of it.
Looks like Hank is stealing your thunder, Lightning.

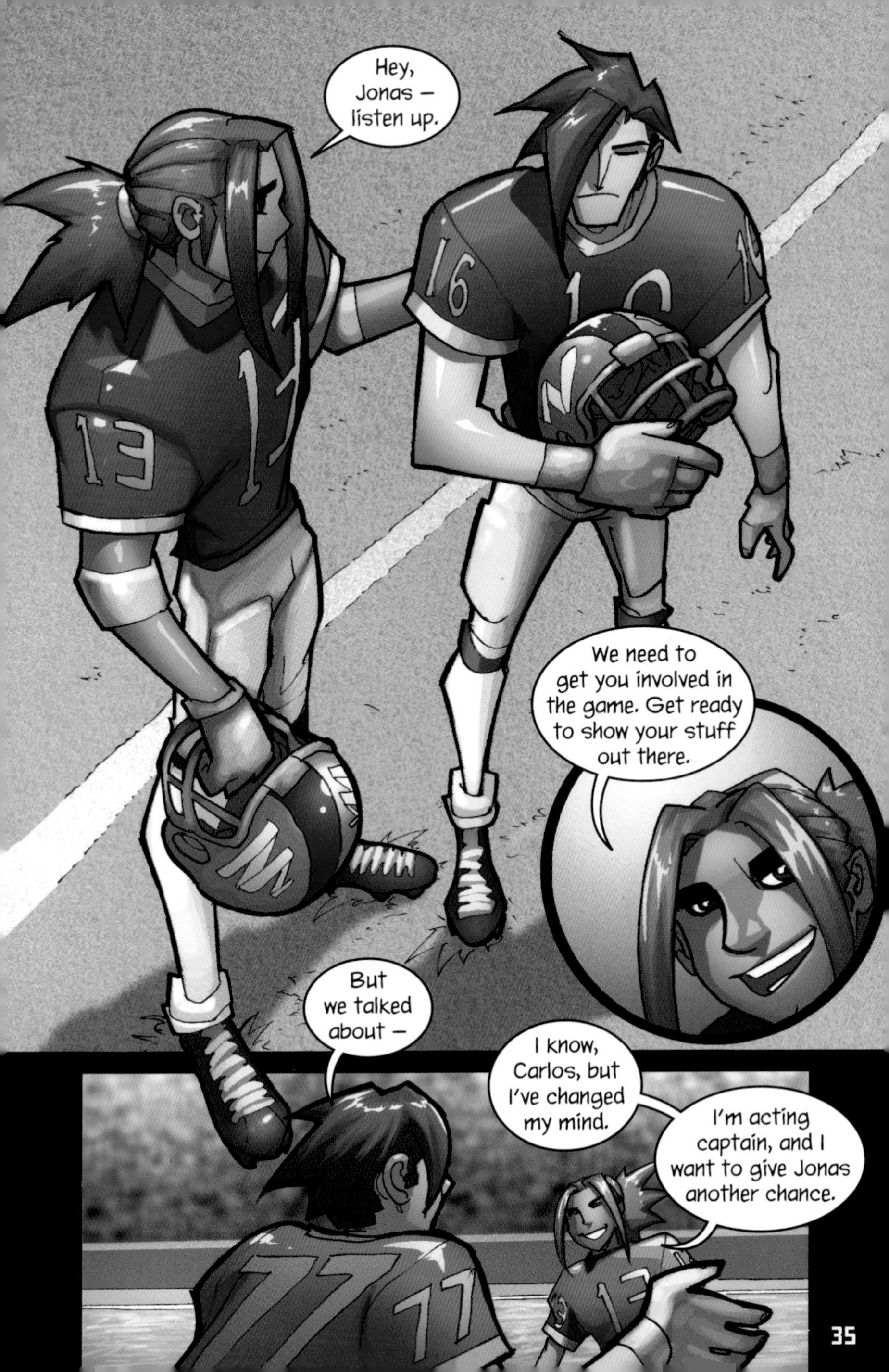
Hey, Jonas — listen up.
We need to get you involved in the game. Get ready to show your stuff out there.
But we talked about —
I know, Carlos, but I've changed my mind.
I'm acting captain, and I want to give Jonas another chance.

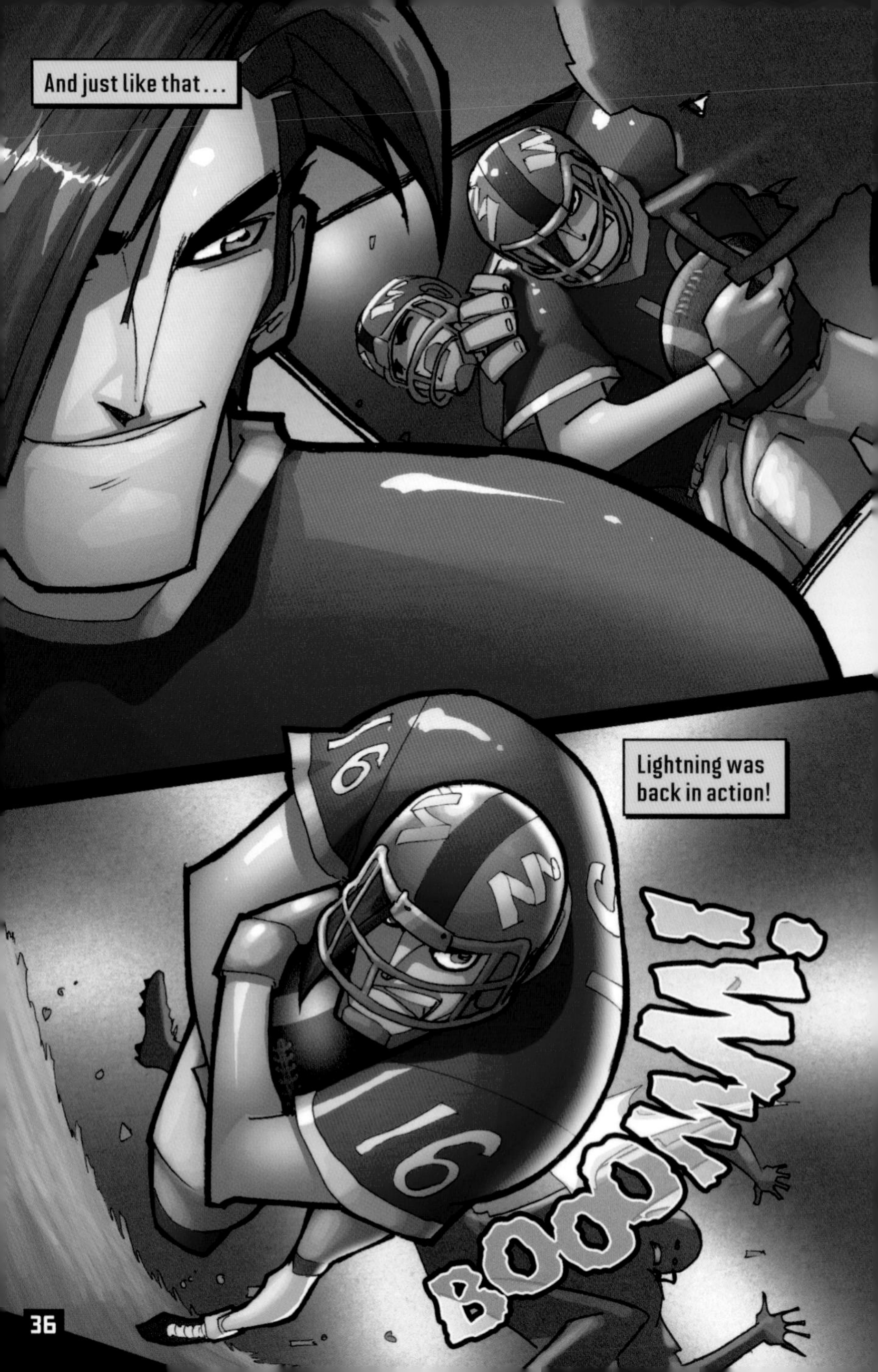
And just like that . . .
Lightning was back in action!
BOOOM!

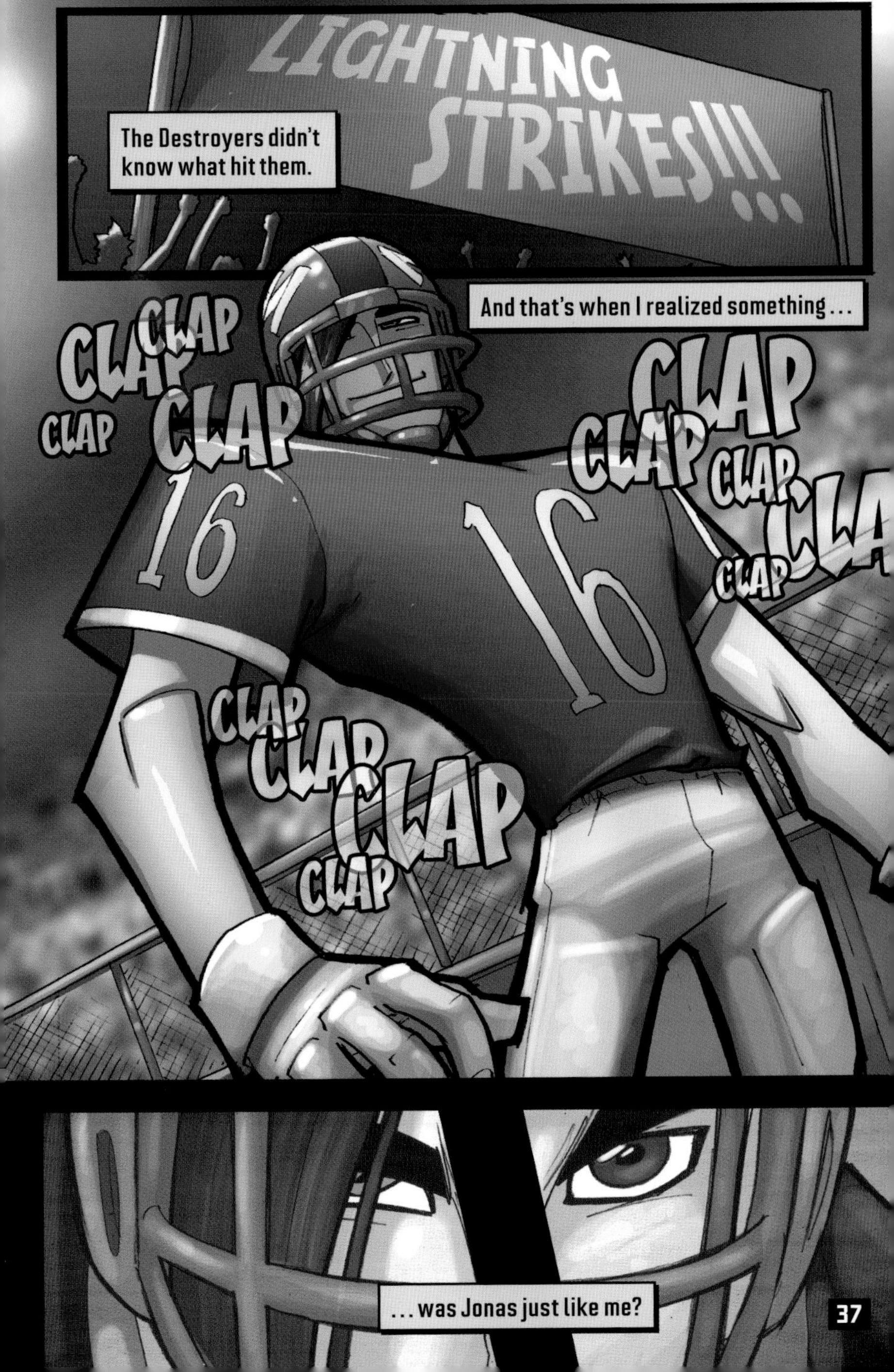
LIGHTNING STRIKES!!! ...
The Destroyers didn't know what hit them.
And that's when I realized something . . .
CLAP CLAP CLAP CLAP
CLAP CLAP CLAP CLAP
CLAP CLAP
CLAP CLAP CLAP CLAP
. . . was Jonas just like me?

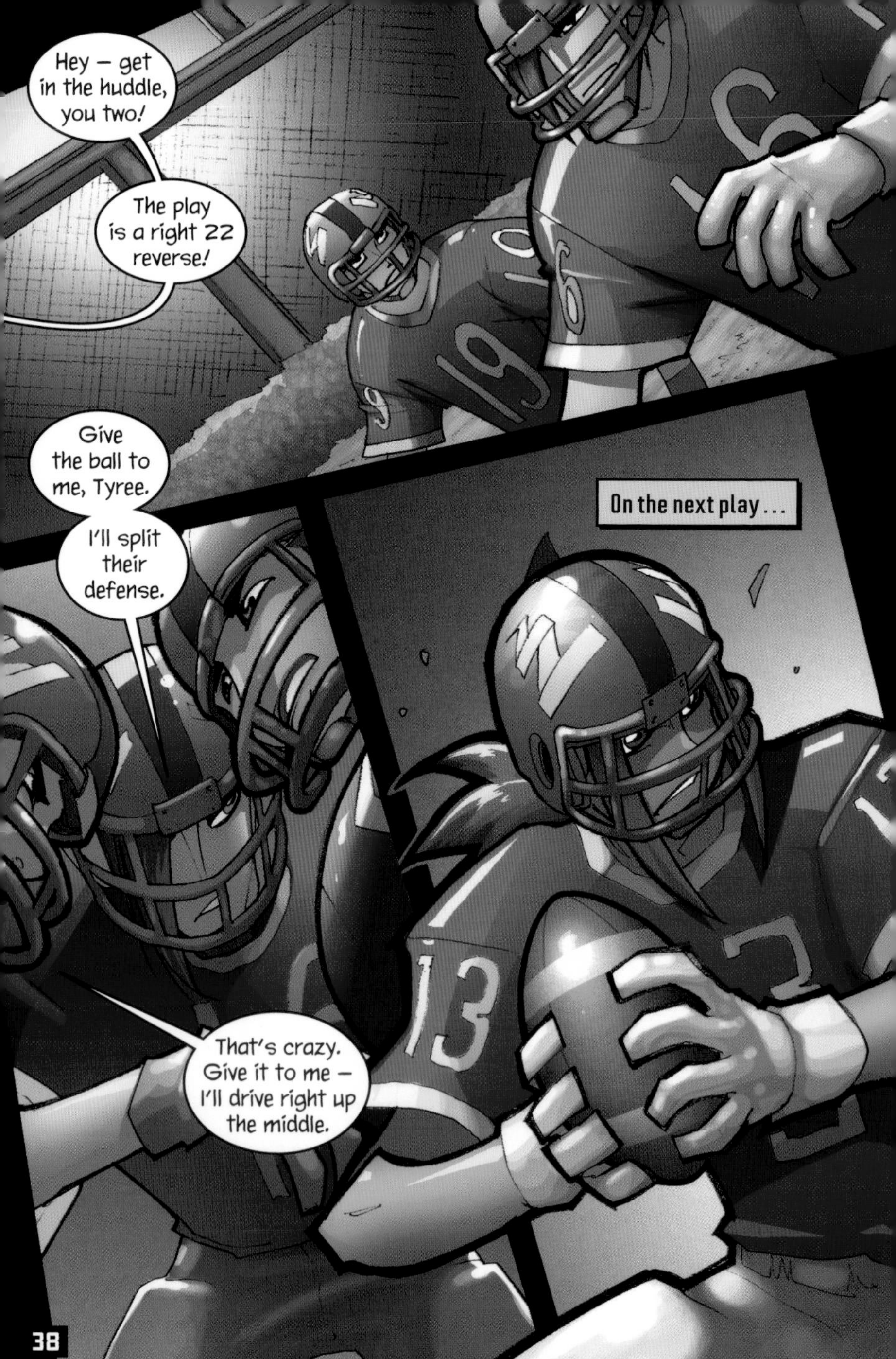

Hey — get in the huddle, you two!
The play is a right 22 reverse!
Give the ball to me, Tyree.
I'll split their defense.
That's crazy. Give it to me — I'll drive right up the middle.
On the next play . . .

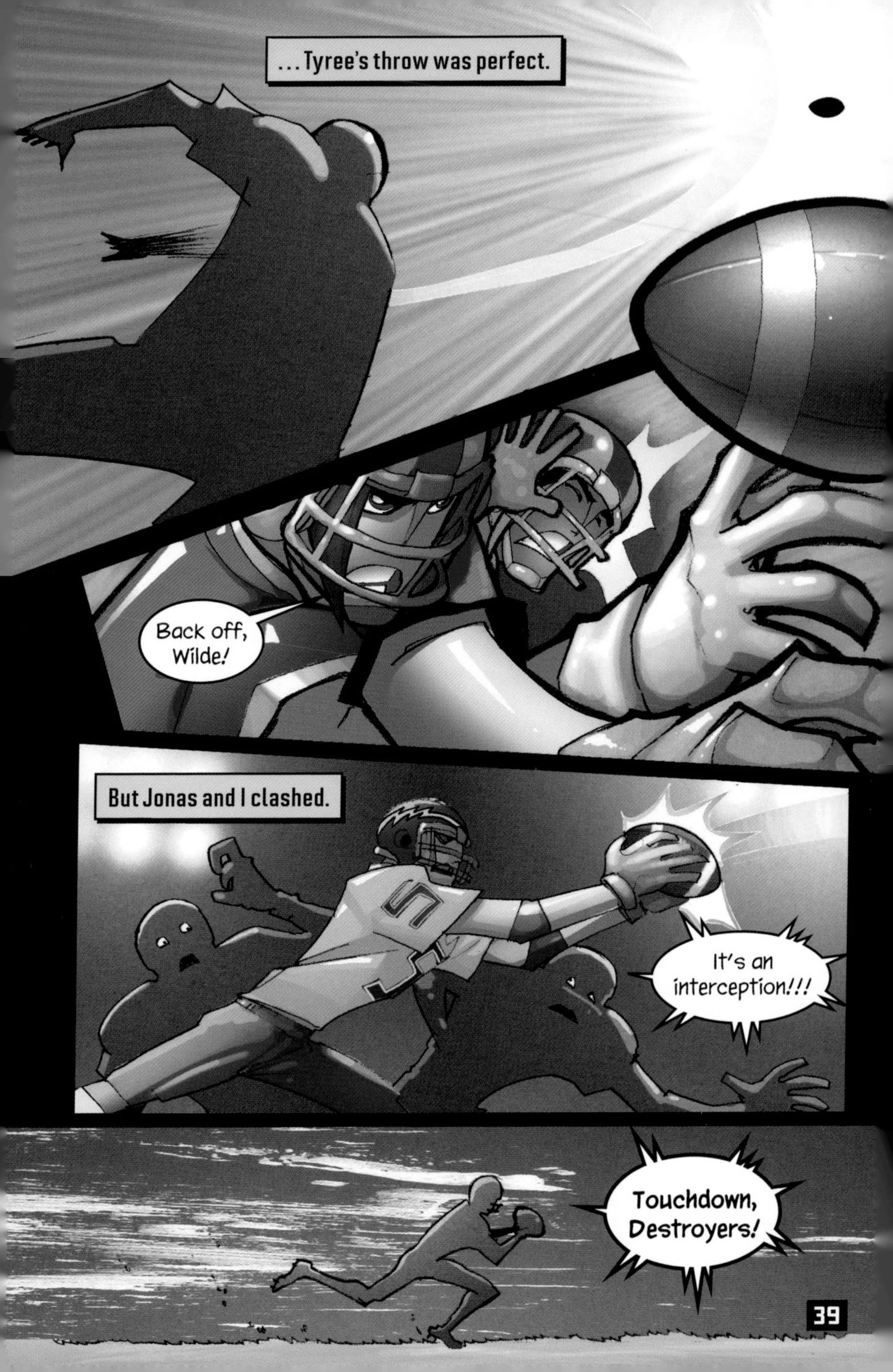
. . . Tyree's throw was perfect.
Back off, Wilde!
But Jonas and I clashed.
It's an interception!!!
Touchdown, Destroyers!

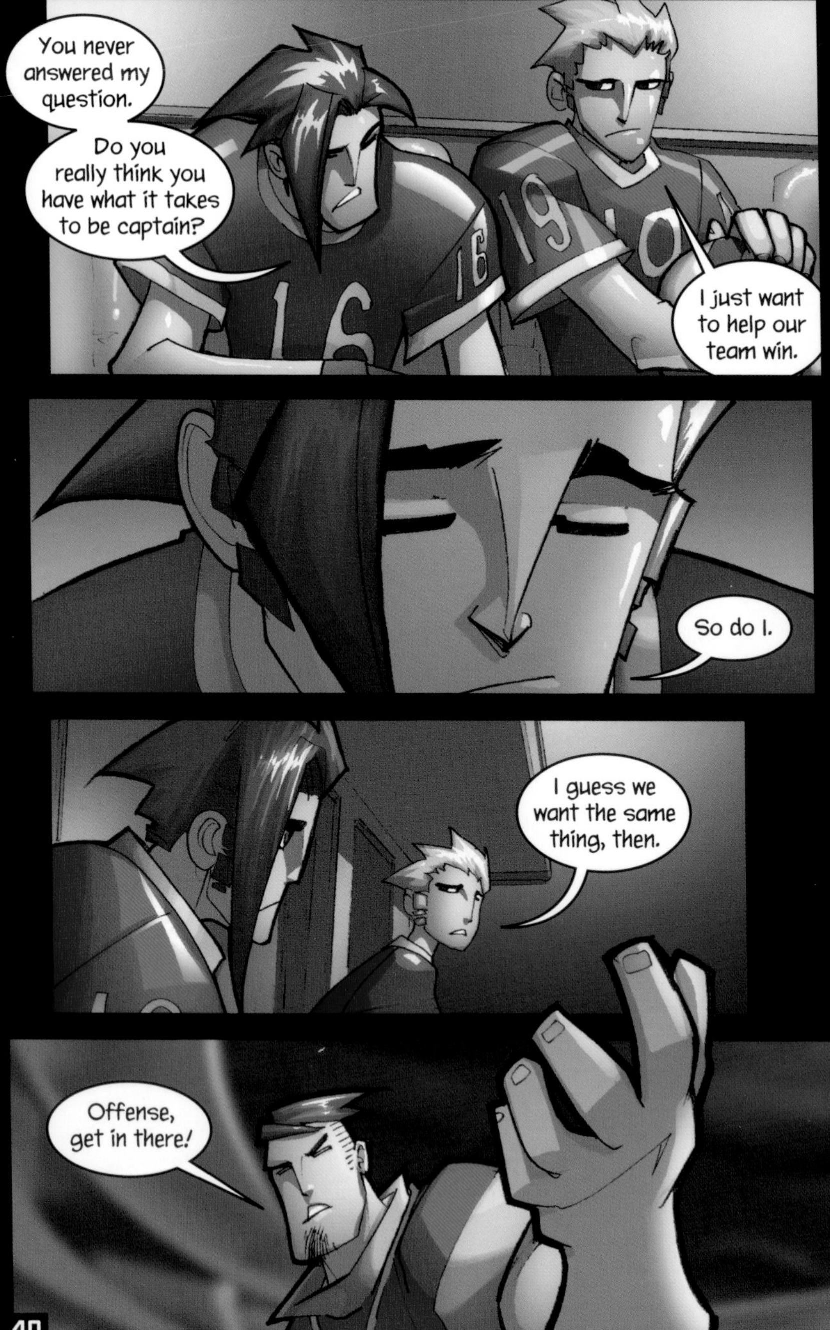
You never answered my question.
Do you really think you have what it takes to be captain?
I just want to help our team win.
So do I.
I guess we want the same thing, then.
Offense, get in there!

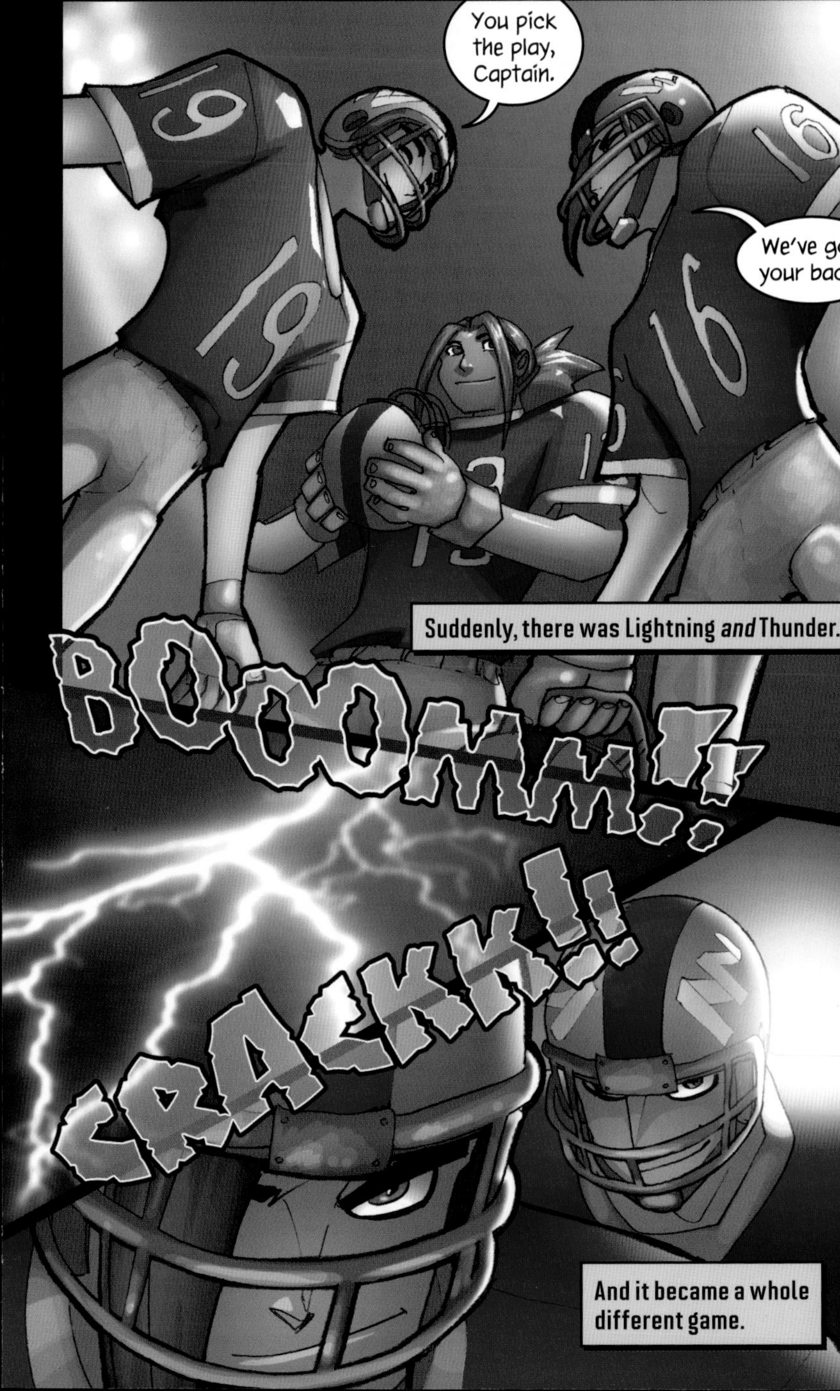
You pick the play, Captain.
We've got your back.
Suddenly, there was Lightning *and* Thunder.
BOOOMM!!
CRACKK!!
And it became a whole different game.

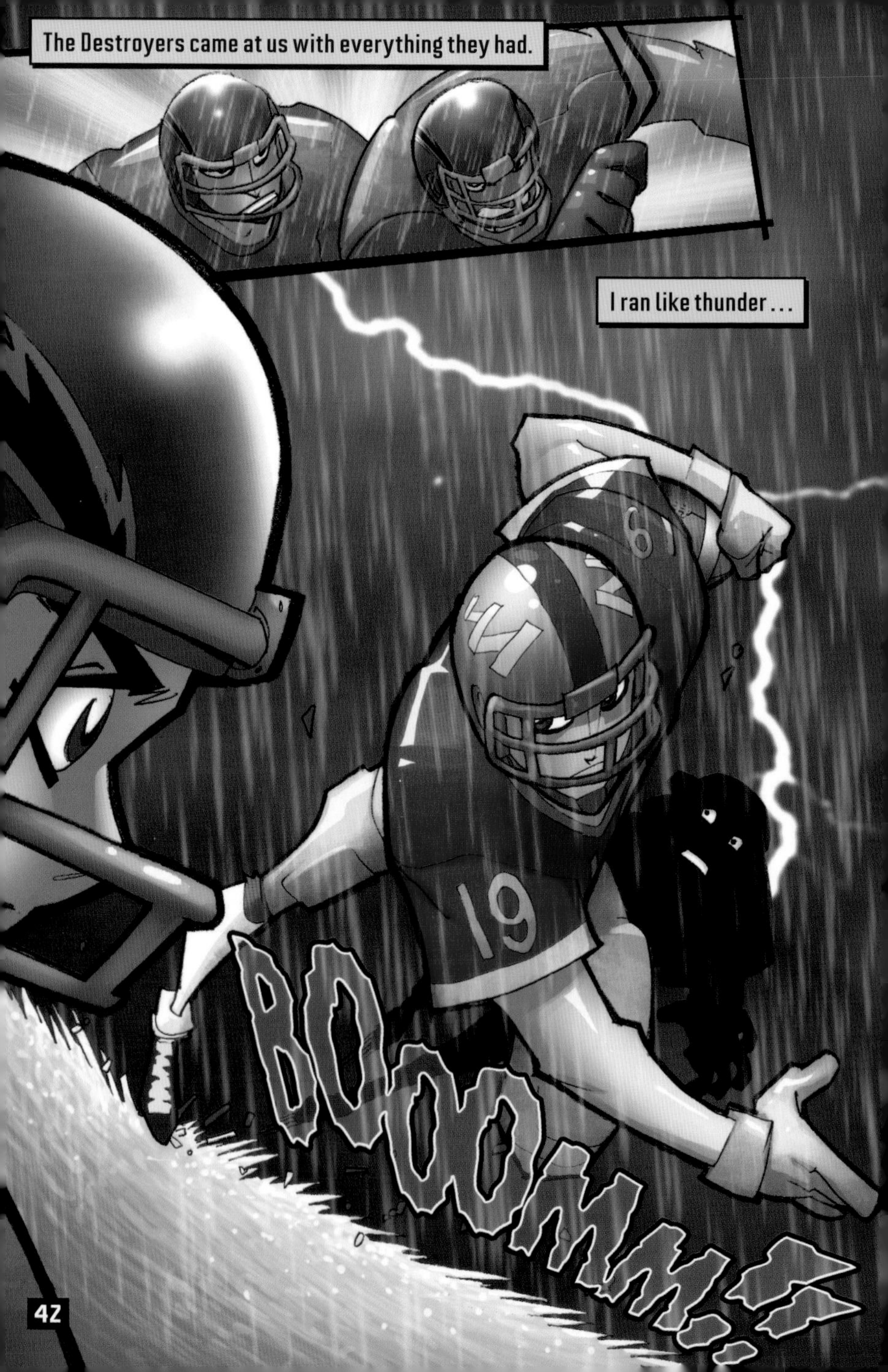

The Destroyers came at us with everything they had.
I ran like thunder . . .
19
BOOOMM!!

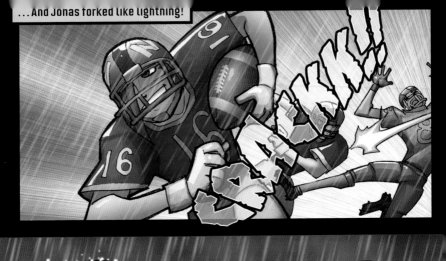

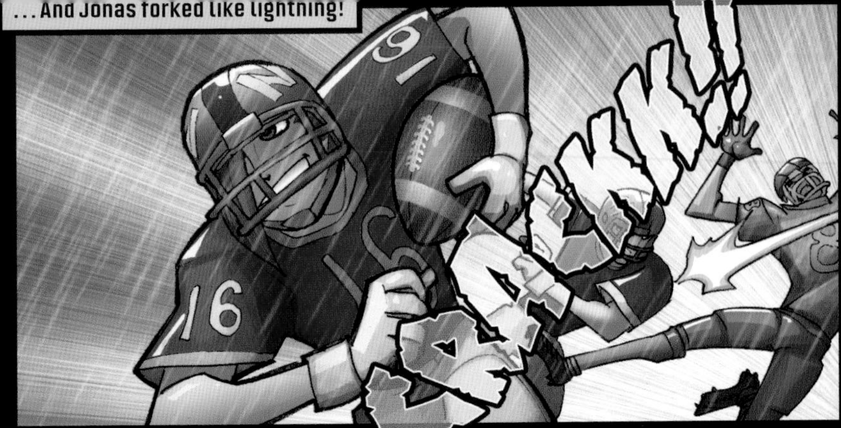
...And Jonas forked like lightning!

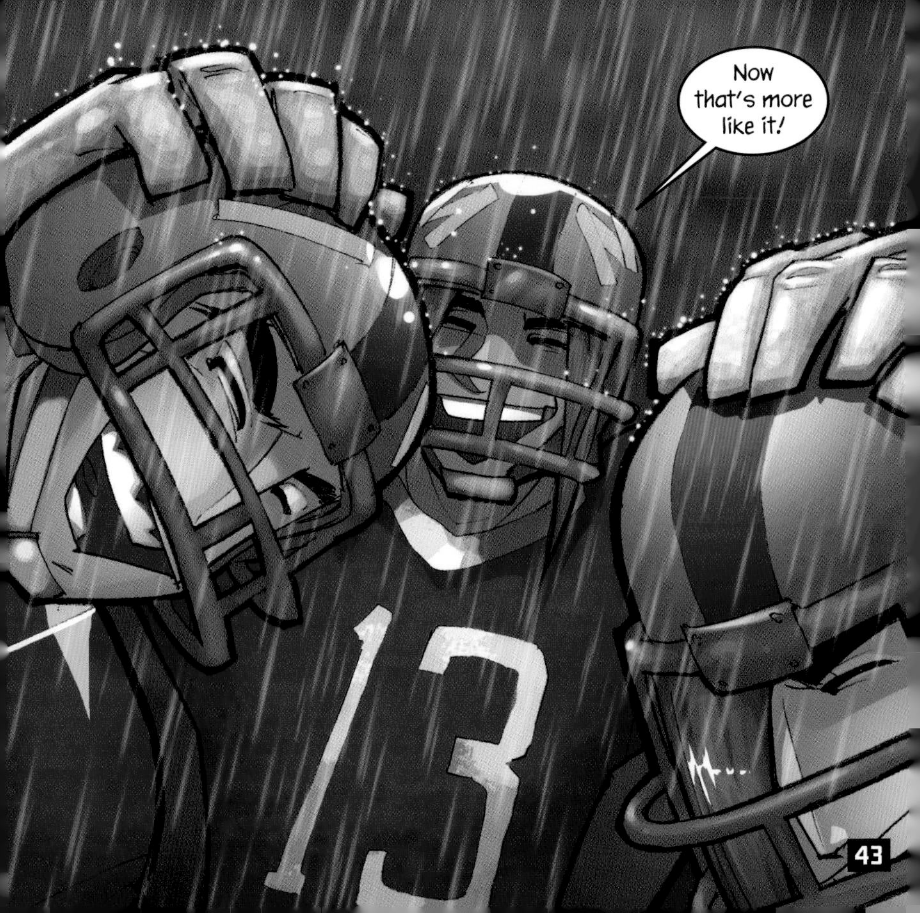
Now that's more like it!

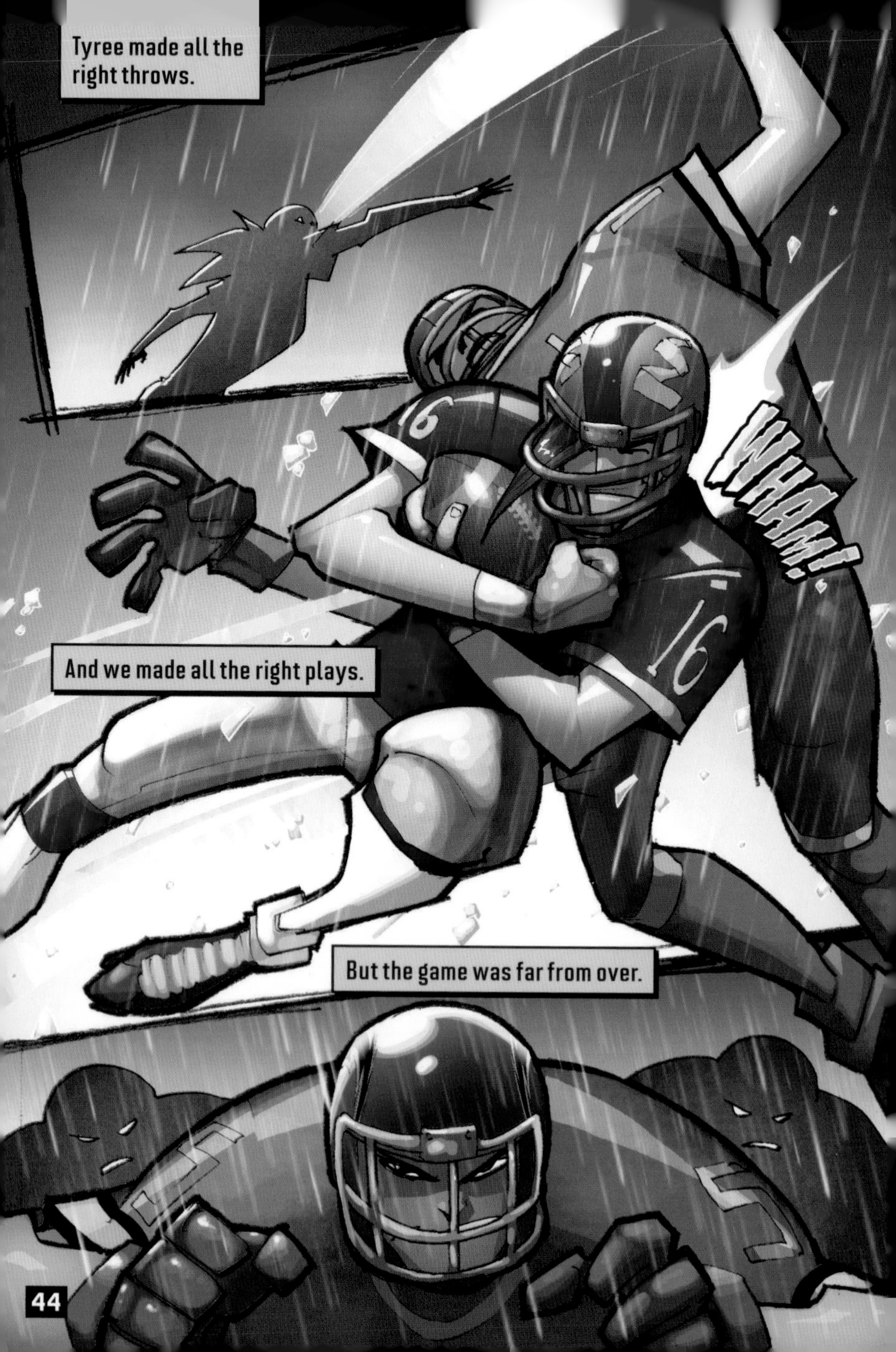
Tyree made all the right throws.
WHAM!
And we made all the right plays.
But the game was far from over.

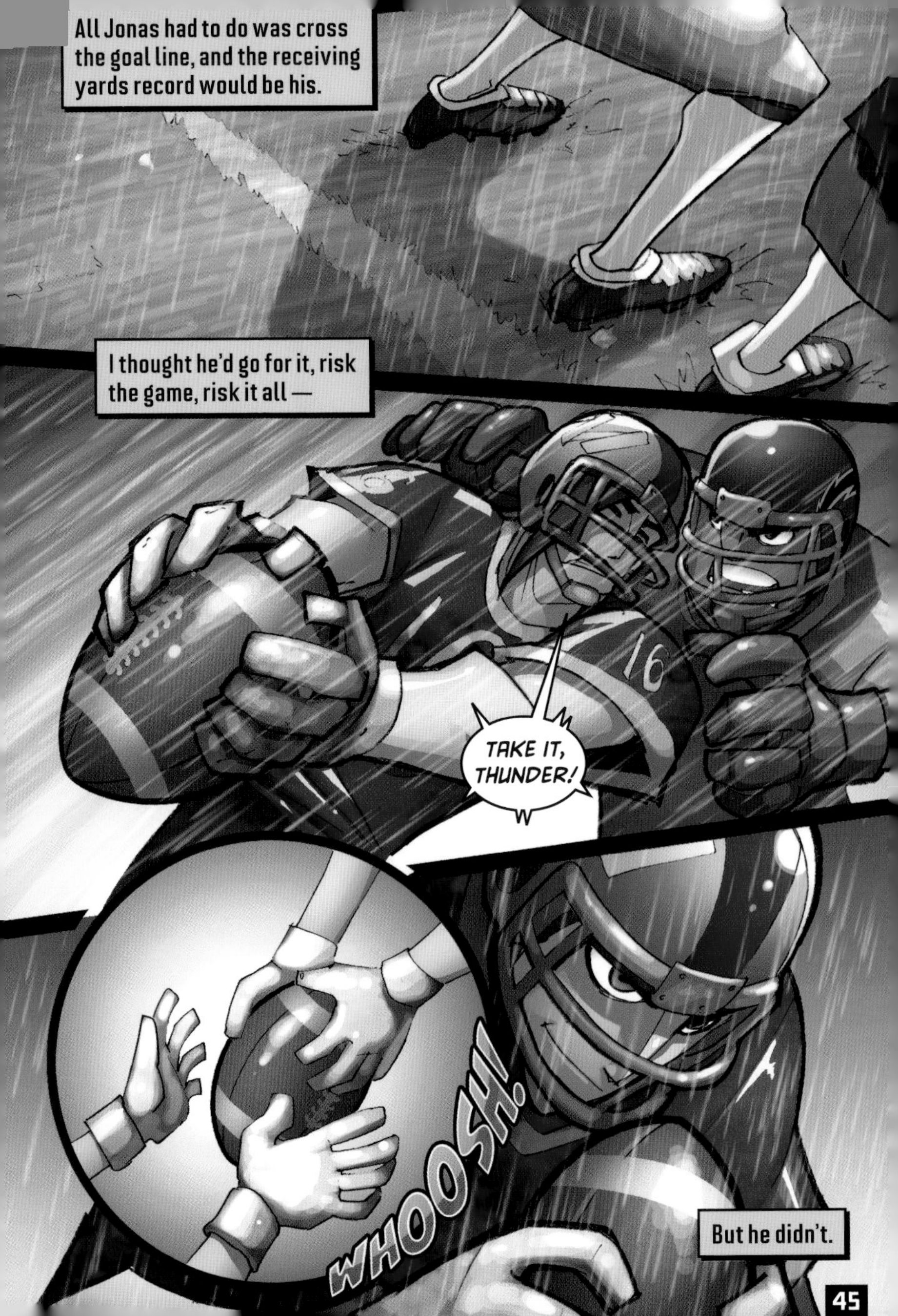
All Jonas had to do was cross the goal line, and the receiving yards record would be his.
I thought he'd go for it, risk the game, risk it all —
TAKE IT, THUNDER!
WHOOSH!
But he didn't.

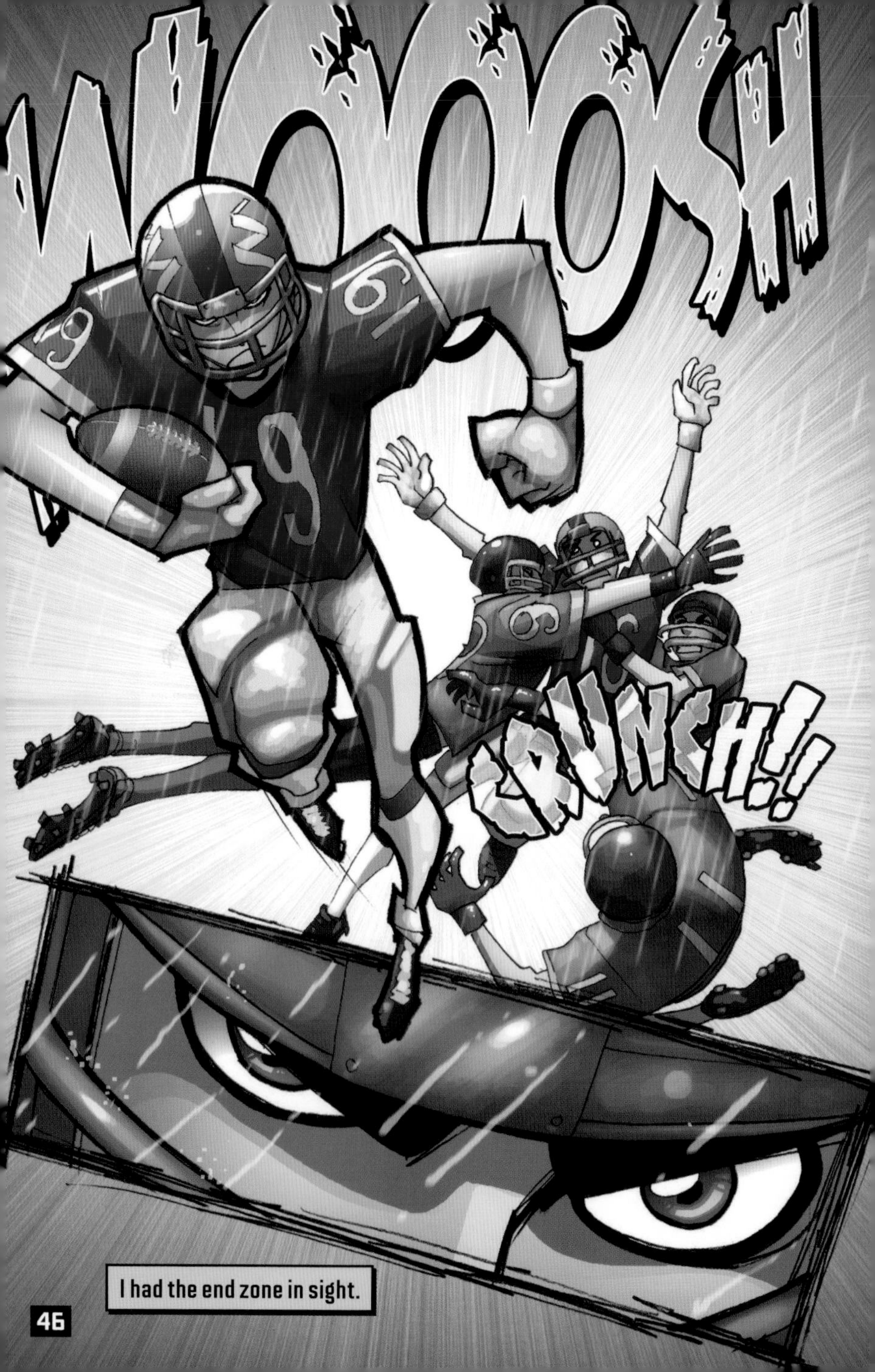
CRUNCH!!
I had the end zone in sight.

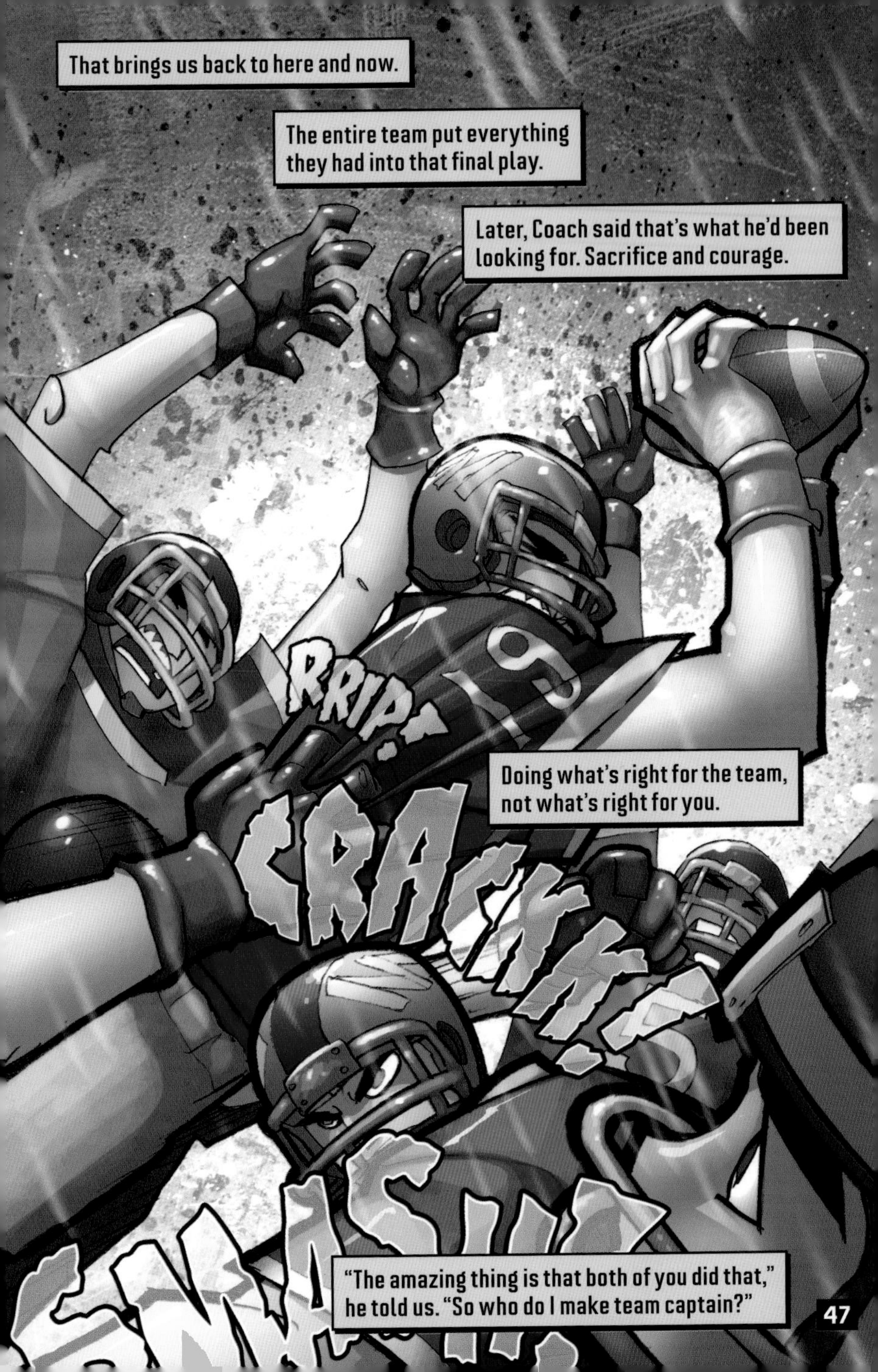

That brings us back to here and now.
The entire team put everything they had into that final play.
Later, Coach said that's what he'd been looking for. Sacrifice and courage.
RRIP!
Doing what's right for the team, not what's right for you.
CRACK!
"The amazing thing is that both of you did that," he told us. "So who do I make team captain?"

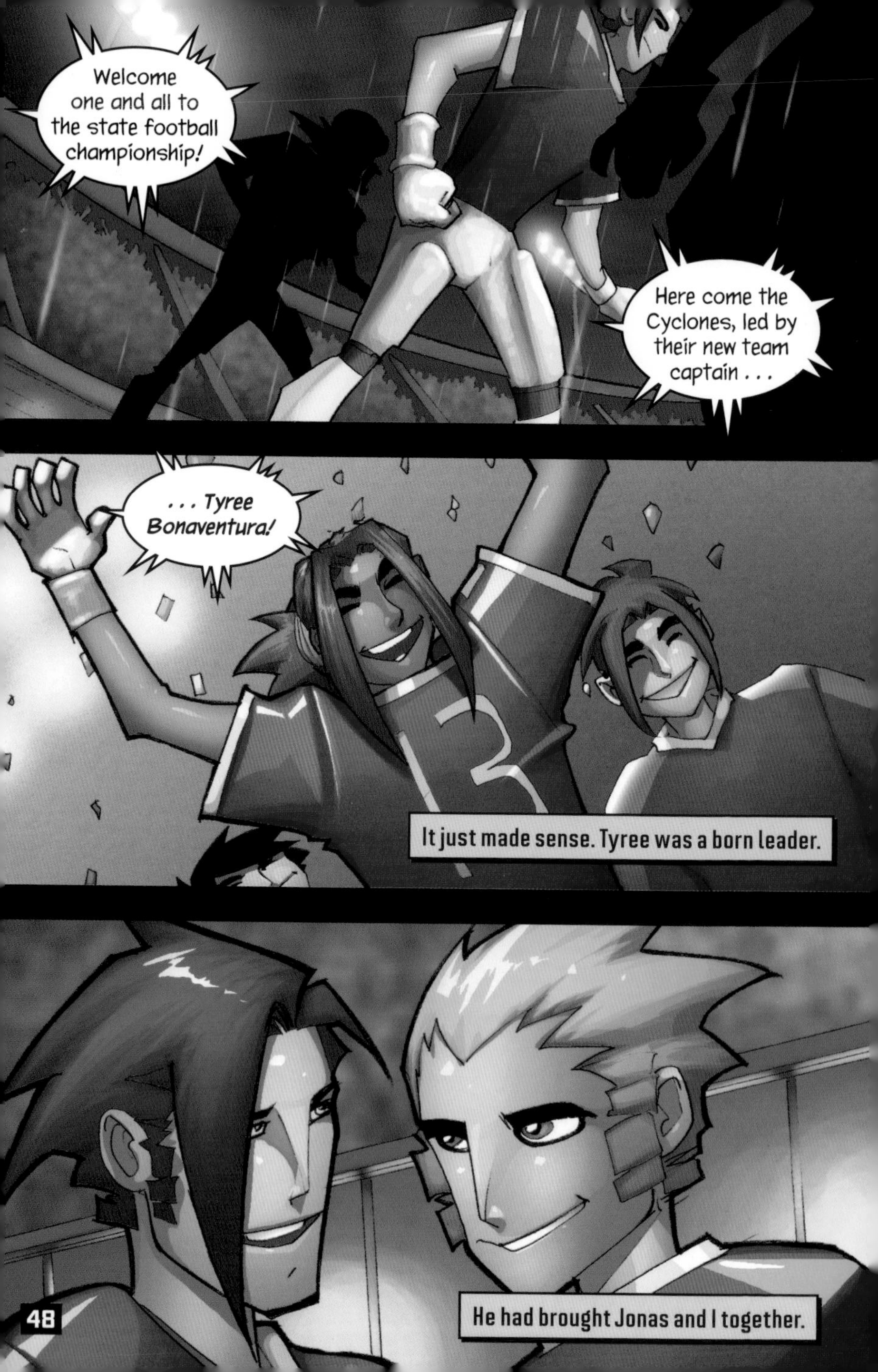
Welcome one and all to the state football championship!
Here come the Cyclones, led by their new team captain . . .
. . . Tyree Bonaventura!
It just made sense. Tyree was a born leader.
He had brought Jonas and I together.

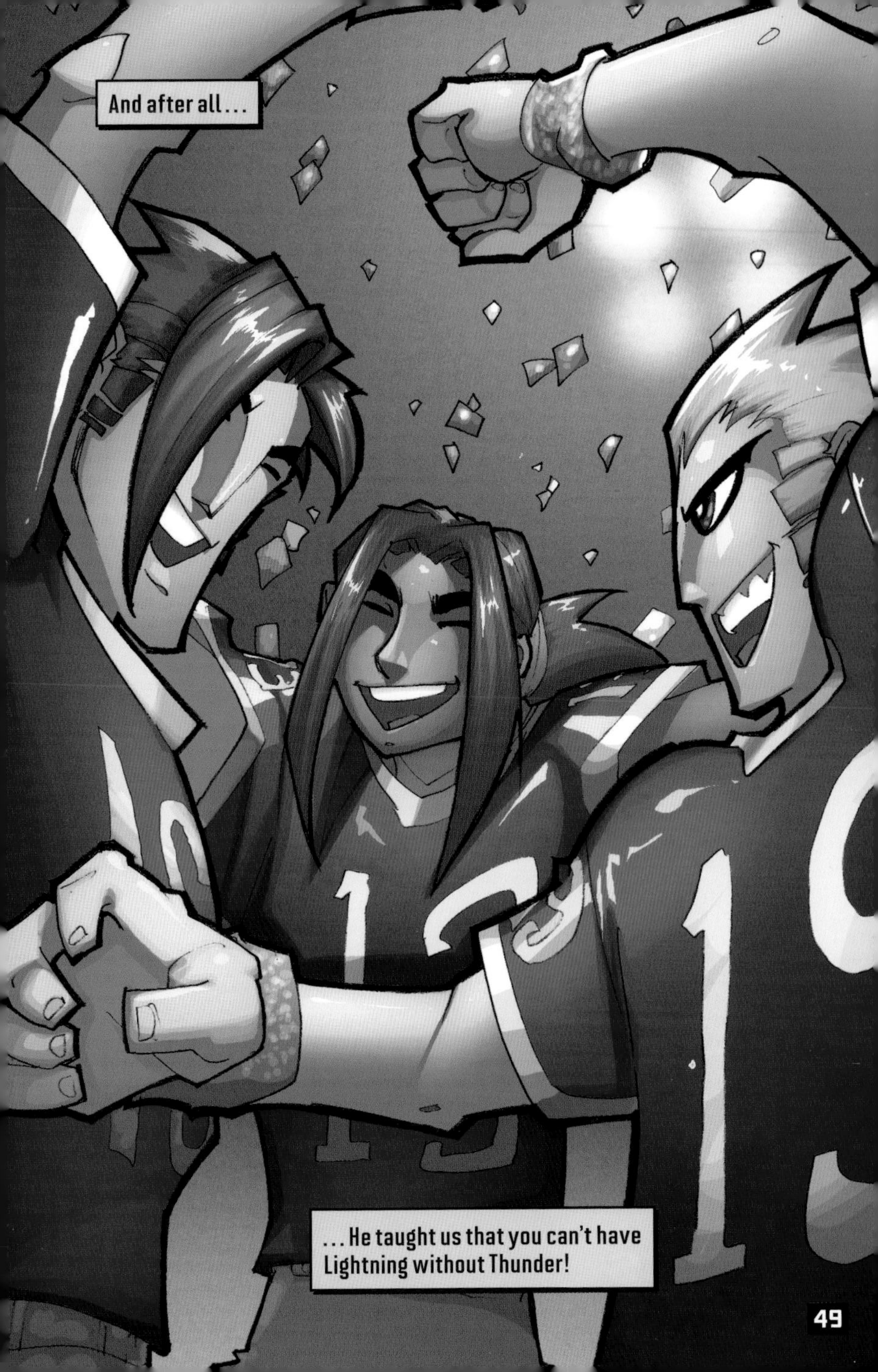
And after all . . .
. . . He taught us that you can't have Lightning without Thunder!

PORTS ZONE

TGAME RECAP

"THUNDER" AND "LIGHTNING" TEAM UP TO CREATE PERFECT OFFENSIVE STORM!

THE
IBERS

YARDS:
212
: 179

:
EZ: 3

STORY: The Cyclones will be playing for the state title this year after a stellar playoff run. The post-season surge featured a three-headed offensive monster that struck fear into their overwhelmed opponents. Hank Wilde and Jonas Fine teamed up for 391 all-purpose yards in the big victory, while Tyree Bonaventura hooked up with the two receivers for two touchdowns apiece.

ports
strated KIDS

UP NEXT: SI KIDS INFO CENTER

SZ *POSTGAME EXTRA*
WHERE *YOU* ANALYZE THE GAME!

BLZ vs BKS
3-1
TGR vs ROR
33-32
EAG vs BAN
14-7
SPA vs WLD
4-3
BAN vs ROR
21-15
RZR vs LIG
4-3

Football fans got a real treat today when Jonas and Hank ran wild on the Destroyers. Let's go into the stands and ask some fans for their opinions on the day's big game …

DISCUSSION QUESTION 1

Can teammates also be enemies? Is it good to compete with your friends? Discuss your answers.

DISCUSSION QUESTION 2

Who is your favorite Cyclone — Hank Wilde, Jonas Fine, Tyree Bonaventura, Tou Yang, or Carlos Ramirez? Why?

WRITING PROMPT 1

Have you ever competed for something? What were you trying to win? How did it turn out? Write about your competitive experience.

WRITING PROMPT 2

Rewrite the ending to this story. What happens to Hank and Jonas? Does Tyree still become captain? You decide.

INFO CENTER

GLOSSARY

DETERMINED   (di-TUR-mind)—if you are determined to do something, you have made a firm decision to do it

EXHAUSTED   (eg-ZAWST-id)—very tired

INTERCEPTION   (in-tur-SEP-shuhn)—a pass that is caught by an opposing player that gives possession of the ball to his team

QUARTERBACK   (KWAWR-tur-bak)—the player on offense who directs the team's plays by way of handoffs or passes

REALIZED   (REE-uh-lized)—became aware that something was true

WIDE RECEIVER   (WIDE ree-SEE-vur)—an offensive player who specializes in catching passes

CREATORS

SCOTT CIENCIN › *Author*

Scott Ciencin is a *New York Times* bestselling author of children's and adult fiction. He has written comic books, trading cards, video games, television shows, as well as many non-fiction projects. He lives in Sarasota, Florida with his beloved wife, Denise, and his best buddy, Bear, a golden retriever. He loves writing books for Stone Arch and is working hard on many more that are still to come.

GERARDO SANDOVAL › *Illustrator*

Gerardo Sandoval is a professional comic book illustrator from Mexico. He has worked on many well-known comics including the Tomb Raider books from Top Cow Productions. He has also worked on designs for posters and card sets.

BENNY FUENTES › *Colorist*

Benny Fuentes lives in Villahermosa, Tabasco in Mexico, where it's just as hot as the sauce is. He studied graphic design in college, but now he works as a full-time colorist in the comic book industry for companies like Marvel, DC Comics, and Top Cow Productions. He shares his home with two crazy cats, Chelo and Kitty, who act like they own the place.

Sports Illustrated KIDS GRAPHIC NOVELS

QUICK COMIC

TOU YANG IN:

KICKOFF BLITZ

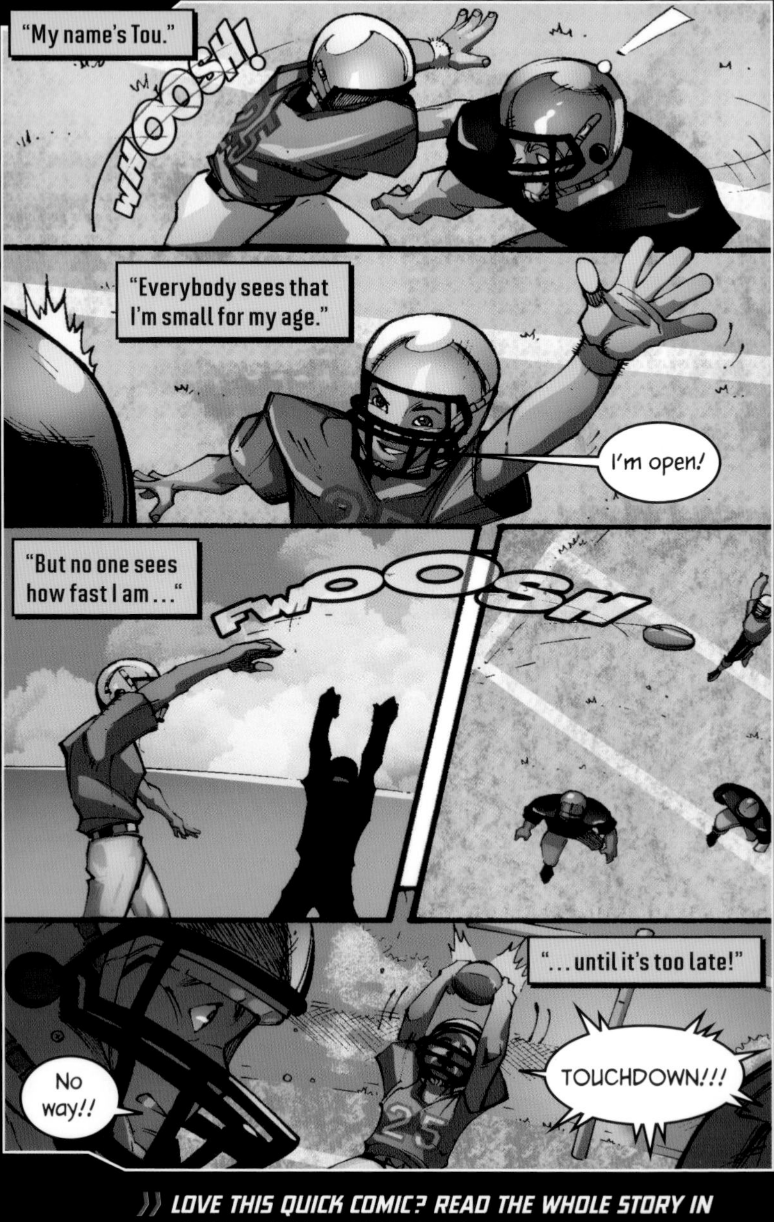
"My name's Tou."
WHOOOSH!
"Everybody sees that I'm small for my age."
I'm open!
"But no one sees how fast I am . . ."
FWOOOSH
". . . until it's too late!"
No way!!
TOUCHDOWN!!!

LOVE THIS QUICK COMIC? READ THE WHOLE STORY IN KICKOFF BLITZ – ONLY FROM STONE ARCH BOOKS!

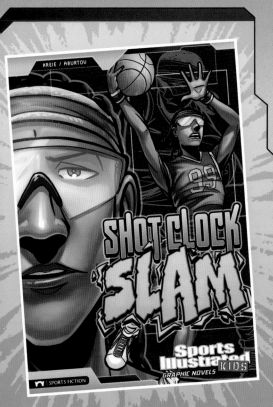